LEGO NINJAGO

Masters of Spinjitzu

Masters of Spinjitzu

MASK OF THE SENSEI

PAPERCUTZ™

LEGO® GRAPHIC NOVELS AVAILABLE FROM PAPERCUTZ™

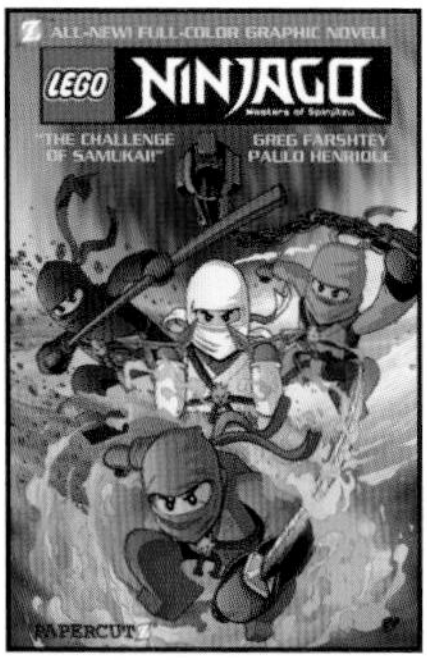
ALL-NEW! FULL-COLOR GRAPHIC NOVEL!
LEGO NINJAGO
"THE CHALLENGE OF SAMUKAI"
GREG FARSHTEY
PAULO HENRIQUE
PAPERCUTZ
NINJAGO #1

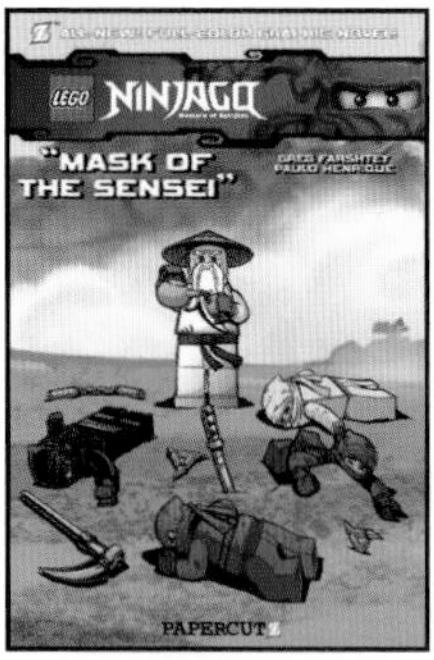
LEGO NINJAGO
"MASK OF THE SENSEI"
PAPERCUTZ
NINJAGO #2

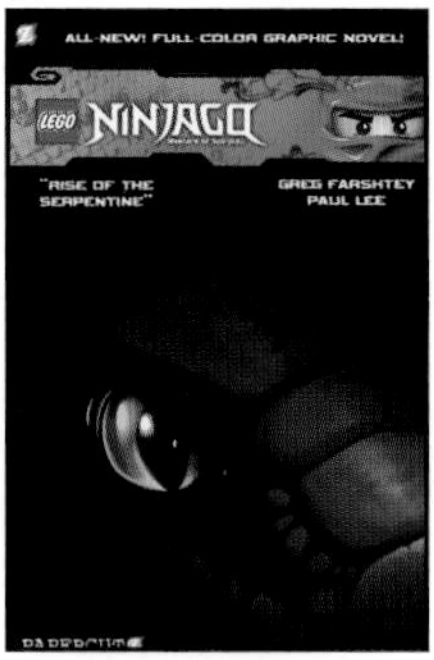
ALL-NEW! FULL COLOR GRAPHIC NOVEL!
LEGO NINJAGO
"RISE OF THE SERPENTINE"
GREG FARSHTEY
PAUL LEE
NINJAGO #3

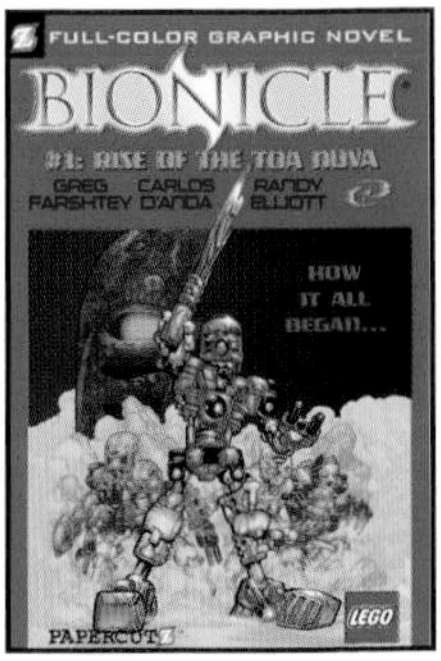
FULL-COLOR GRAPHIC NOVEL
BIONICLE
#1: RISE OF THE TOA NUVA
GREG FARSHTEY
CARLOS D'ANDA
RANDY ELLIOTT
HOW IT ALL BEGAN...
PAPERCUTZ
LEGO
BIONICLE #1

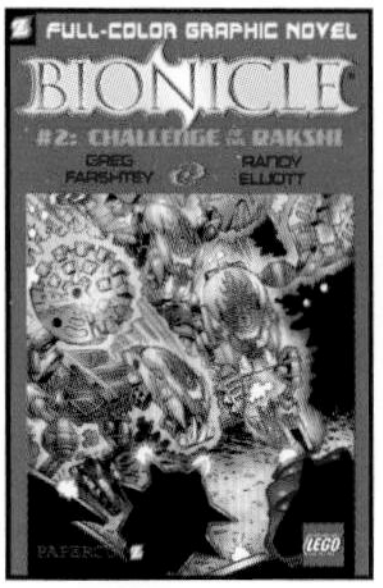
FULL-COLOR GRAPHIC NOVEL
BIONICLE
GREG FARSHTEY
RANDY ELLIOTT
LEGO
BIONICLE #2

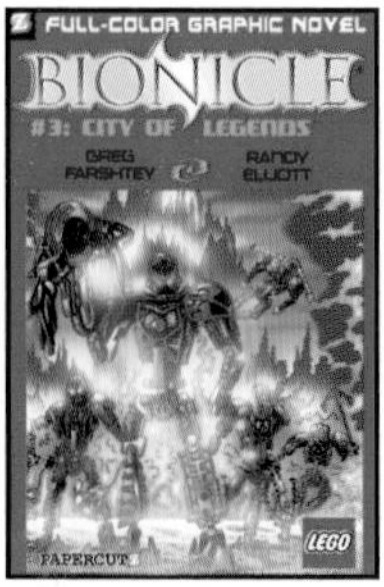
FULL-COLOR GRAPHIC NOVEL
BIONICLE
#3: CITY OF LEGENDS
GREG FARSHTEY
RANDY ELLIOTT
PAPERCUTZ
LEGO
BIONICLE #3

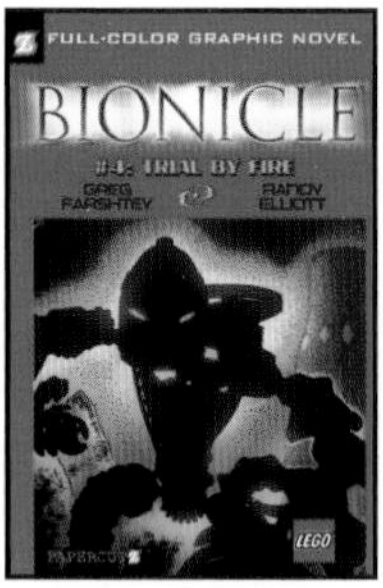
FULL-COLOR GRAPHIC NOVEL
BIONICLE
#4: TRIAL BY FIRE
GREG FARSHTEY
RANDY ELLIOTT
LEGO
BIONICLE #4

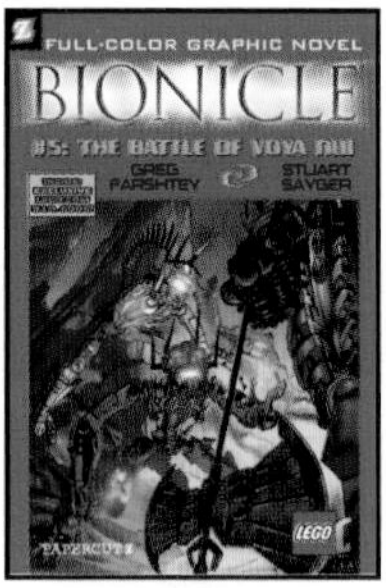
FULL-COLOR GRAPHIC NOVEL
BIONICLE
#5: THE BATTLE OF VOYA NUI
GREG FARSHTEY
STUART SAYGER
LEGO
BIONICLE #5

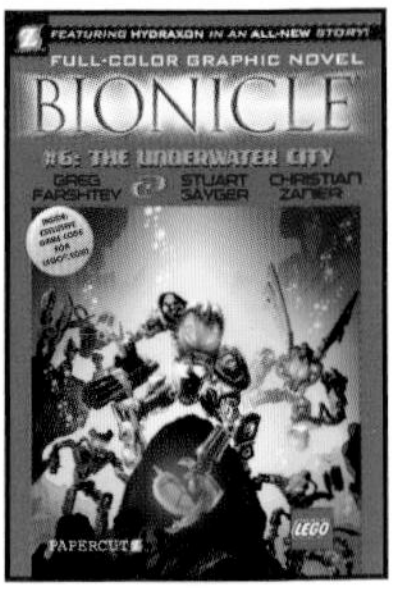
FULL-COLOR GRAPHIC NOVEL
BIONICLE
#6: THE UNDERWATER CITY
GREG FARSHTEY
STUART SAYGER
CHRISTIAN ZANIER
PAPERCUTZ
LEGO
BIONICLE #6

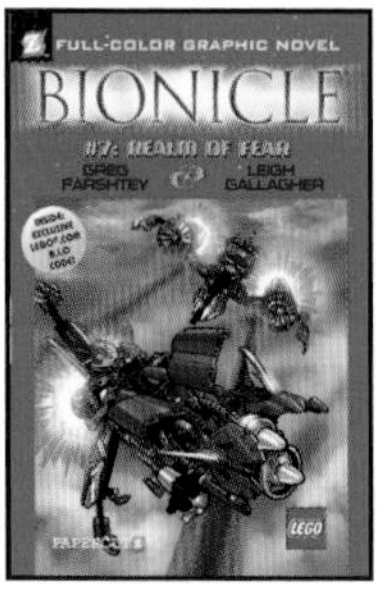
FULL-COLOR GRAPHIC NOVEL
BIONICLE
#7: REALM OF FEAR
GREG FARSHTEY
LEIGH GALLAGHER
LEGO
BIONICLE #7

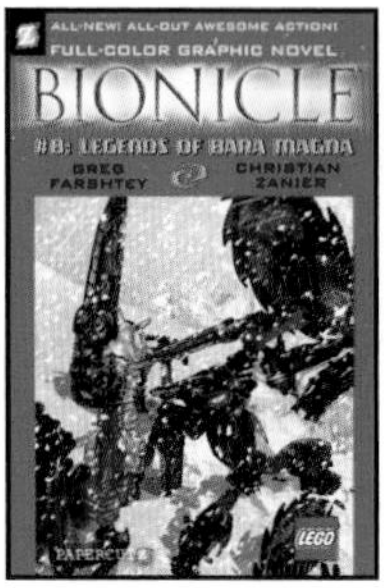
ALL-NEW! ALL-OUT AWESOME ACTION!
FULL-COLOR GRAPHIC NOVEL
BIONICLE
#8: LEGENDS OF BARA MAGNA
GREG FARSHTEY
CHRISTIAN ZANIER
PAPERCUTZ
LEGO
BIONICLE #8

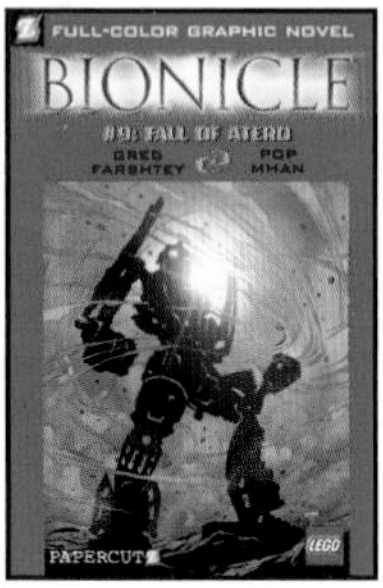
FULL-COLOR GRAPHIC NOVEL
BIONICLE
#9: FALL OF ATERO
GREG FARSHTEY
POP MHAN
PAPERCUTZ
LEGO
BIONICLE #9

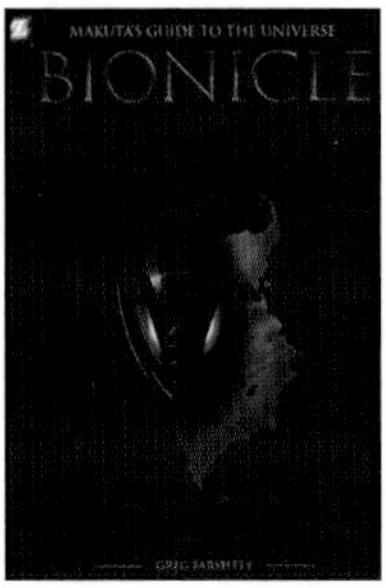
MAKUTA'S GUIDE TO THE UNIVERSE
BIONICLE
Makuta's Guide to the Universe

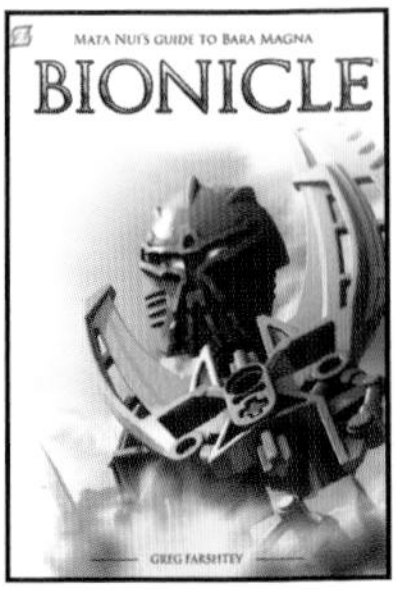
MATA NUI'S GUIDE TO BARA MAGNA
BIONICLE
GREG FARSHTEY
Mata Nui's Guide to Bara Magna

NINJAGO graphic novels, BIONICLE® graphic novels, and guide books are available in paperback and hardcover at booksellers everywhere.

Or order from us: please add $4.00 for postage and handling for first book, add $1.00 for each additional book. NINJAGO #1-3 are $6.99 in paperback, and $13.99 in hardcover. BIONICLE #1-3, 8, and 9 are $8.99 in paperback, $13.99 in hardcover. Guide Books are $9.99 each in paperback only. Please make check payable to NBM Publishing. Send to: Papercutz, 40 Exchange Place, Ste. 1308, New York, NY 10005 • 1-800-886-1223

www.papercutz.com

#2 MASK OF THE SENSEI

GREG FARSHTEY ★ Writer
PAULO HENRIQUE ★ Artist
LAURIE E. SMITH ★ Colorist

New York

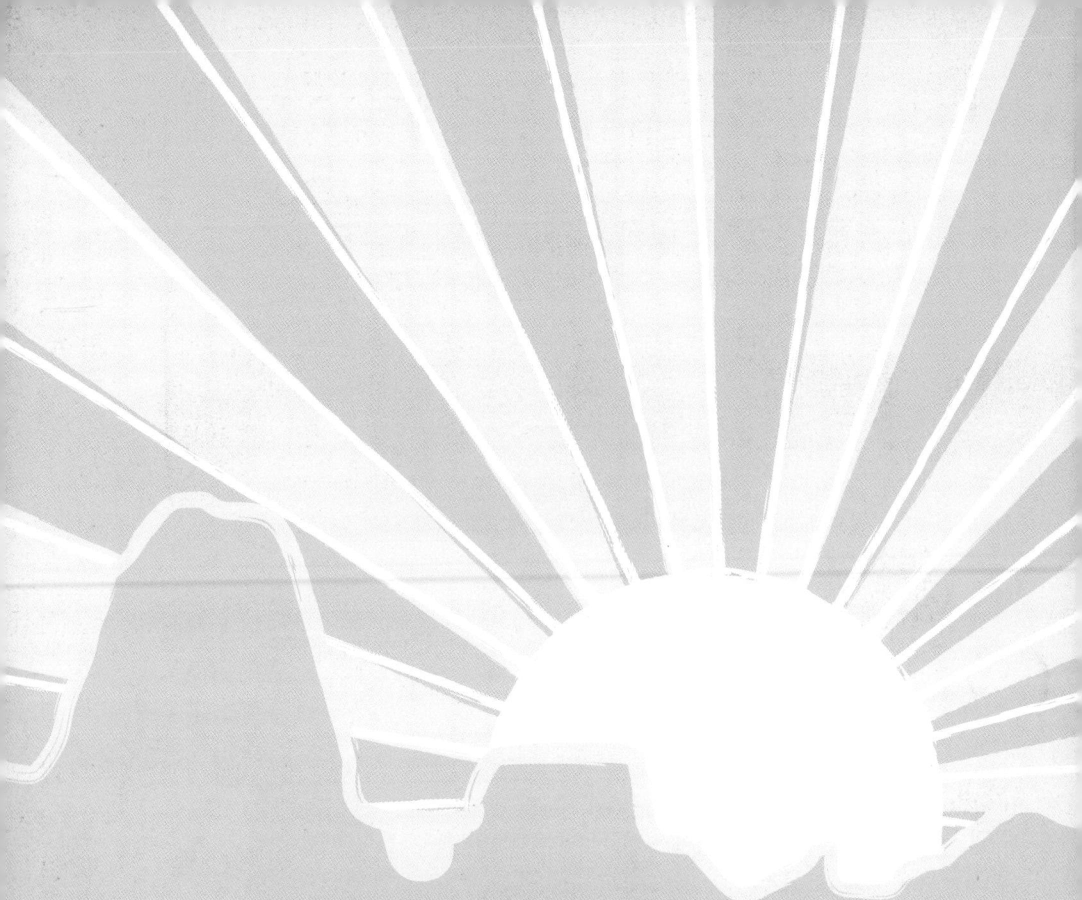

LEGO® NINJAGO Masters of Spinjitsu
#2 "Mask of the Sensei"

GREG FARSHTEY – Writer
PAULO HENRIQUE – Artist
LAURIE E. SMITH – Colorist
BRYAN SENKA – Letterer

Production by Nelson Design Group, LLC
Associate Editor – MICHAEL PETRANEK
JIM SALICRUP
Editor-in-Chief

ISBN: 978-1-59707-310-3 paperback edition
ISBN: 978-1-59707-311-0 hardcover edition

Printed in China
February 2012 by Asia One Printing LTD.
13/F Asia One Tower
8 Fung Yip St., Chaiwan, Hong Kong

Distributed by Macmillan.

First Printing

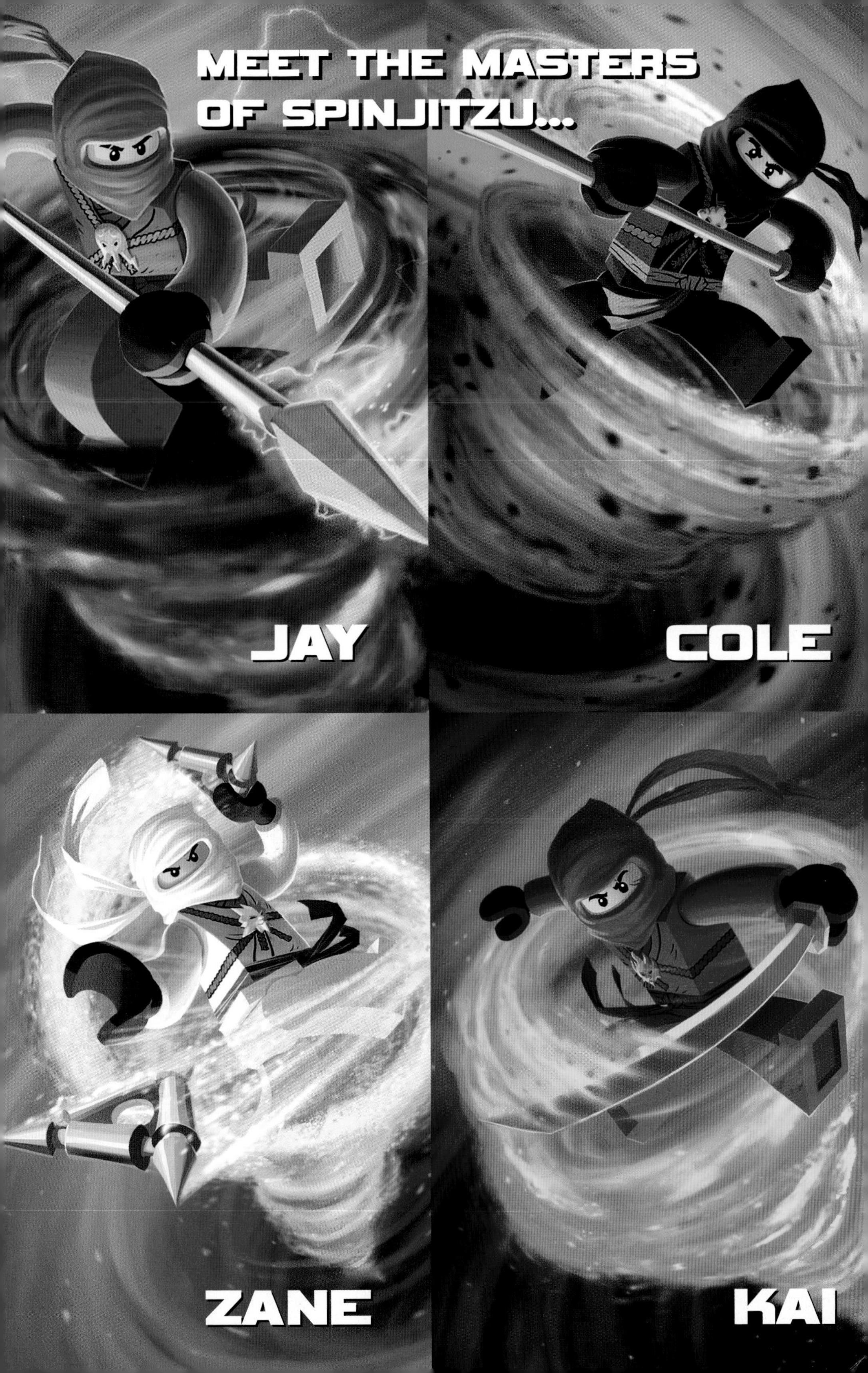
MEET THE MASTERS OF SPINJITZU...
JAY
COLE
ZANE
KAI

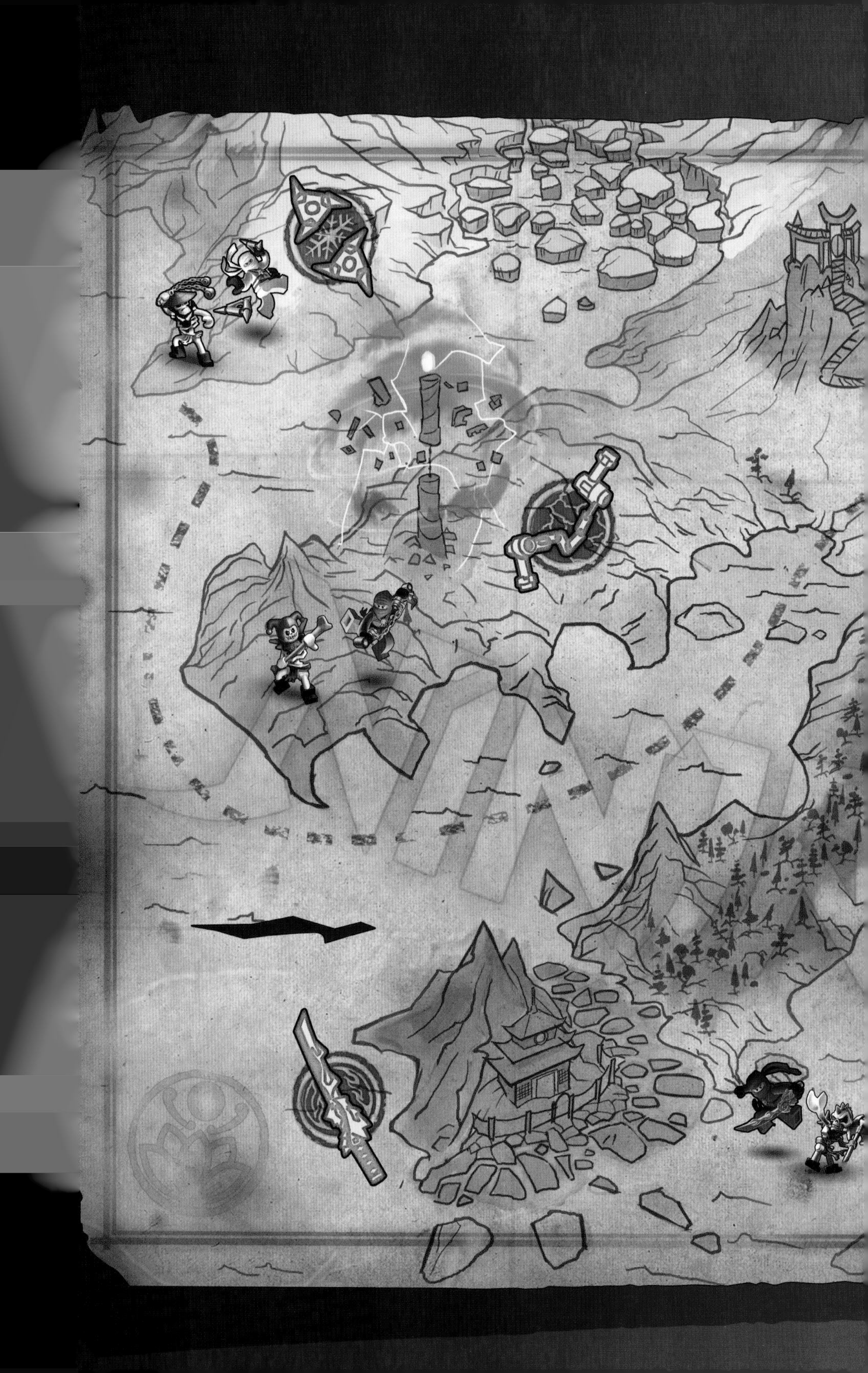

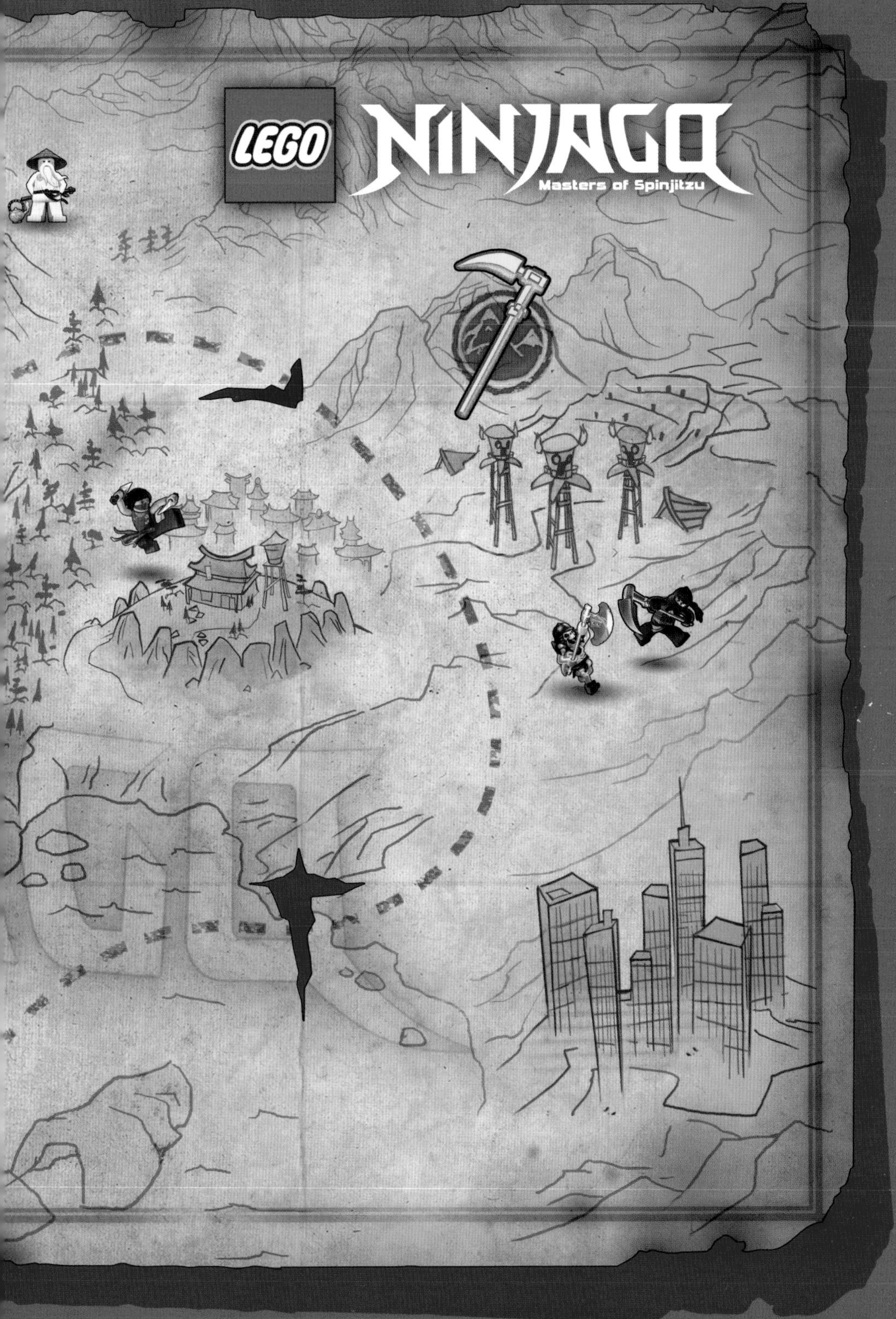
LEGO
NINJAGO
Masters of Spinjitzu

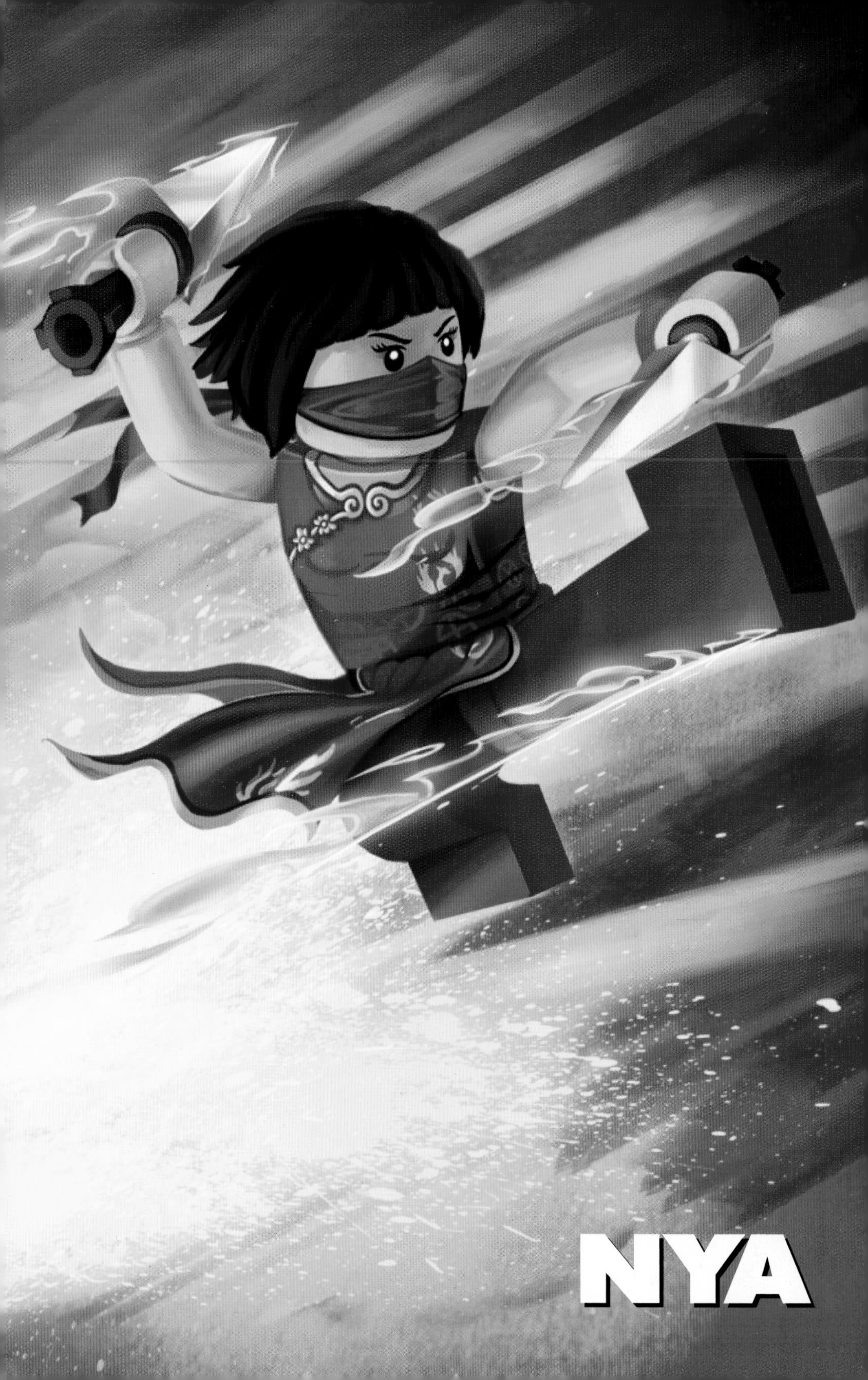
NYA

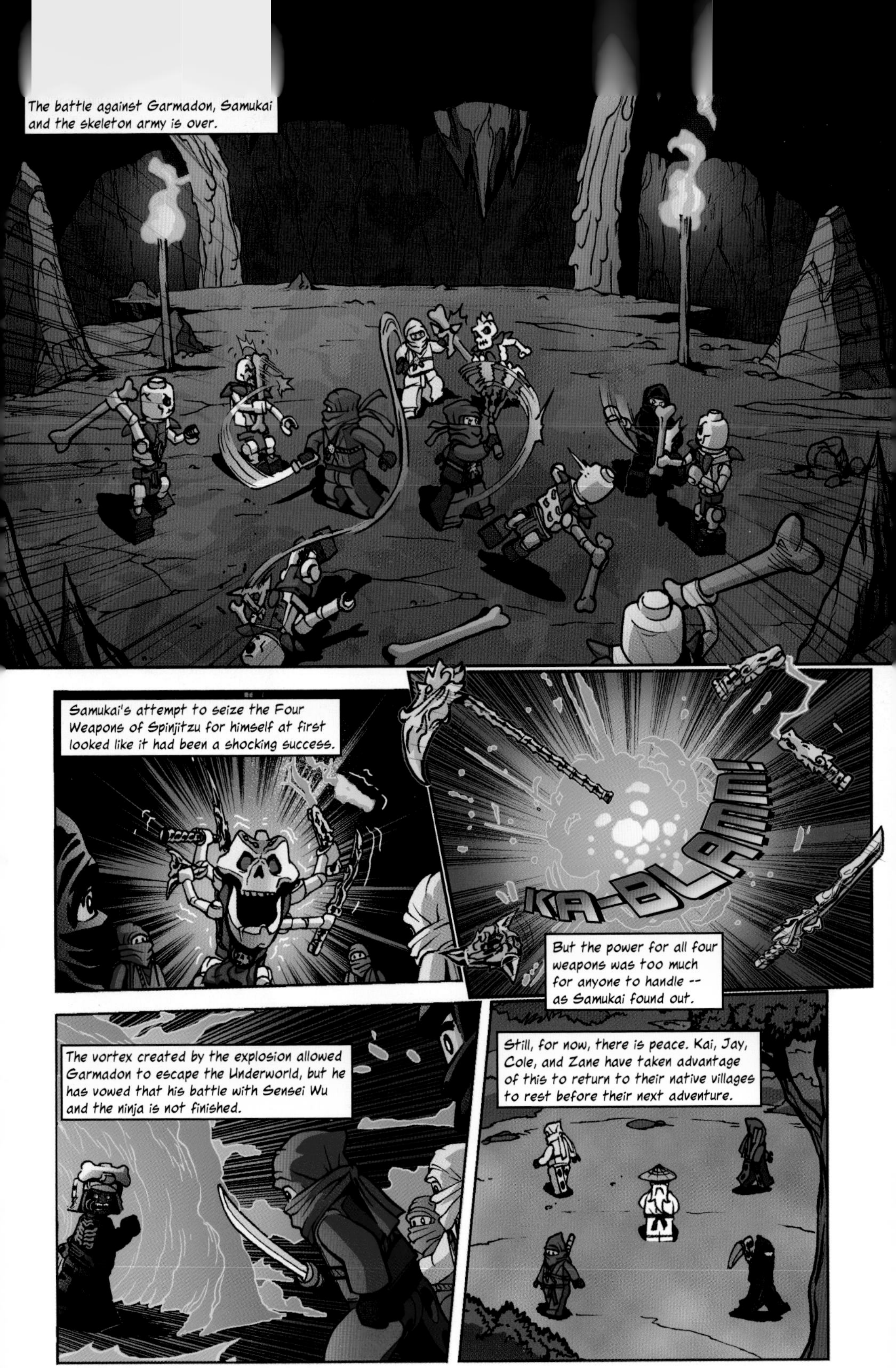
The battle against Garmadon, Samukai and the skeleton army is over.
Samukai's attempt to seize the Four Weapons of Spinjitzu for himself at first looked like it had been a shocking success.
But the power for all four weapons was too much for anyone to handle -- as Samukai found out.
The vortex created by the explosion allowed Garmadon to escape the Underworld, but he has vowed that his battle with Sensei Wu and the ninja is not finished.
Still, for now, there is peace. Kai, Jay, Cole, and Zane have taken advantage of this to return to their native villages to rest before their next adventure.

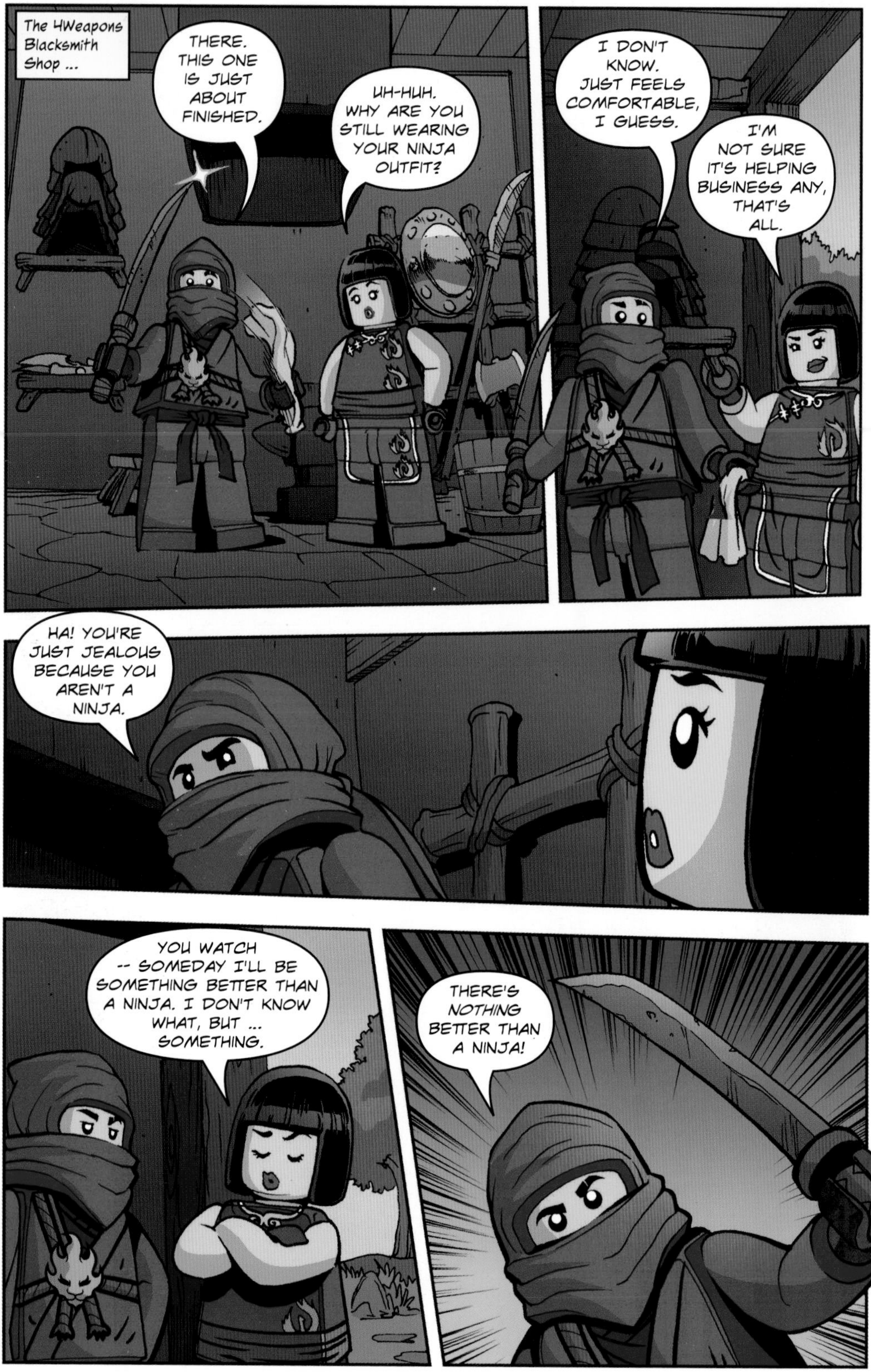
The 4Weapons Blacksmith Shop ...
THERE. THIS ONE IS JUST ABOUT FINISHED.
UH-HUH. WHY ARE YOU STILL WEARING YOUR NINJA OUTFIT?
I DON'T KNOW. JUST FEELS COMFORTABLE, I GUESS.
I'M NOT SURE IT'S HELPING BUSINESS ANY, THAT'S ALL.
HA! YOU'RE JUST JEALOUS BECAUSE YOU AREN'T A NINJA.
YOU WATCH -- SOMEDAY I'LL BE SOMETHING BETTER THAN A NINJA. I DON'T KNOW WHAT, BUT ... SOMETHING.
THERE'S NOTHING BETTER THAN A NINJA!

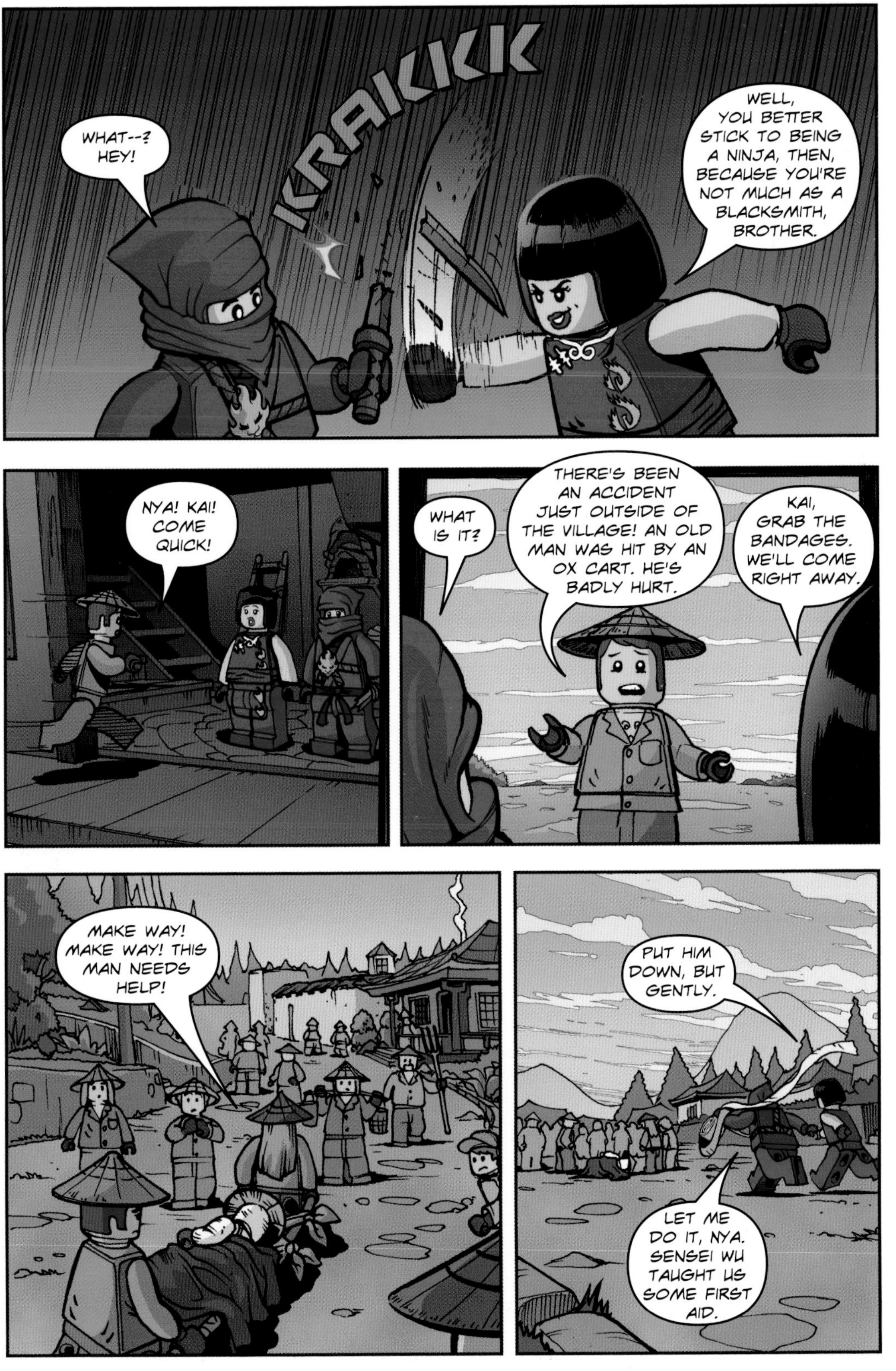
WHAT--? HEY!
KRAKKK
WELL, YOU BETTER STICK TO BEING A NINJA, THEN, BECAUSE YOU'RE NOT MUCH AS A BLACKSMITH, BROTHER.
NYA! KAI! COME QUICK!
WHAT IS IT?
THERE'S BEEN AN ACCIDENT JUST OUTSIDE OF THE VILLAGE! AN OLD MAN WAS HIT BY AN OX CART. HE'S BADLY HURT.
KAI, GRAB THE BANDAGES. WE'LL COME RIGHT AWAY.
MAKE WAY! MAKE WAY! THIS MAN NEEDS HELP!
PUT HIM DOWN, BUT GENTLY.
LET ME DO IT, NYA. SENSEI WU TAUGHT US SOME FIRST AID.

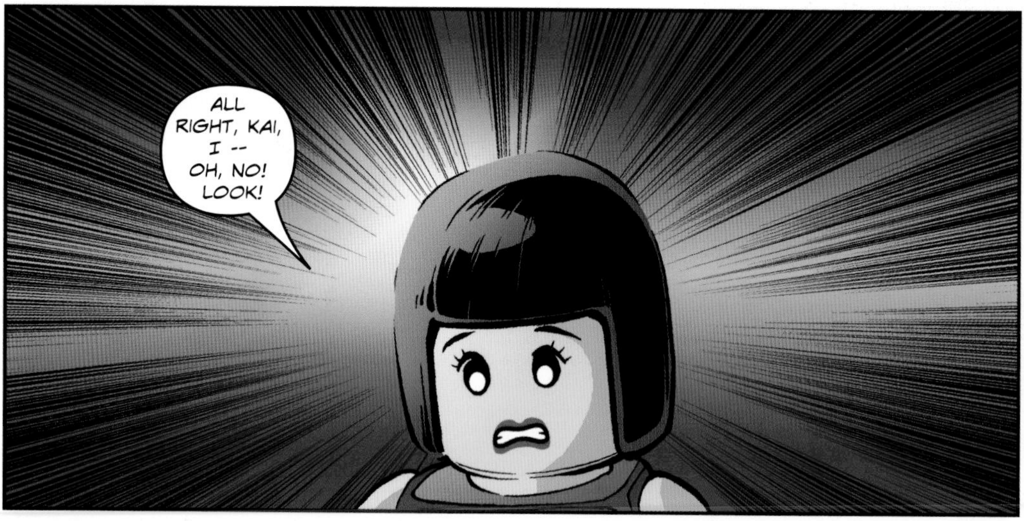
ALL RIGHT, KAI, I -- OH, NO! LOOK!

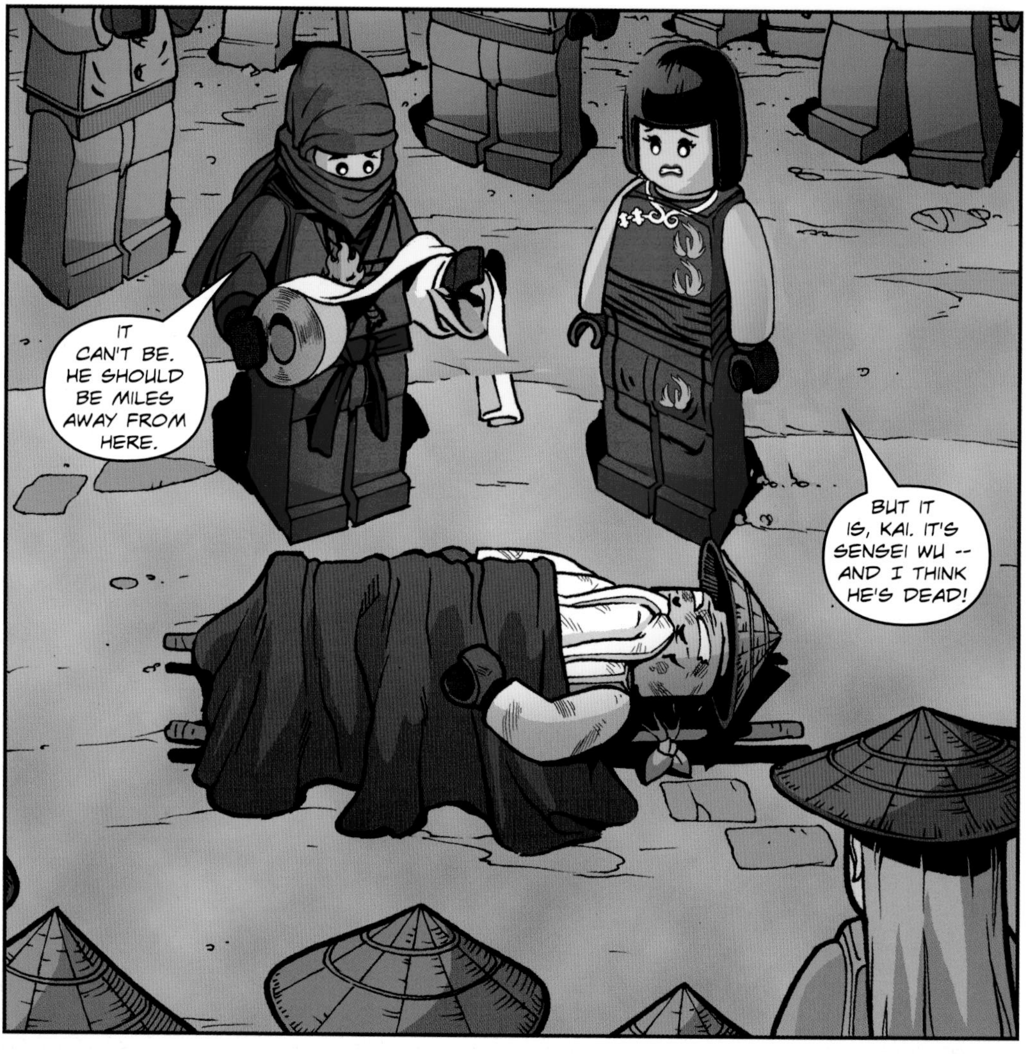
IT CAN'T BE. HE SHOULD BE MILES AWAY FROM HERE.
BUT IT IS, KAI. IT'S SENSEI WU -- AND I THINK HE'S DEAD!

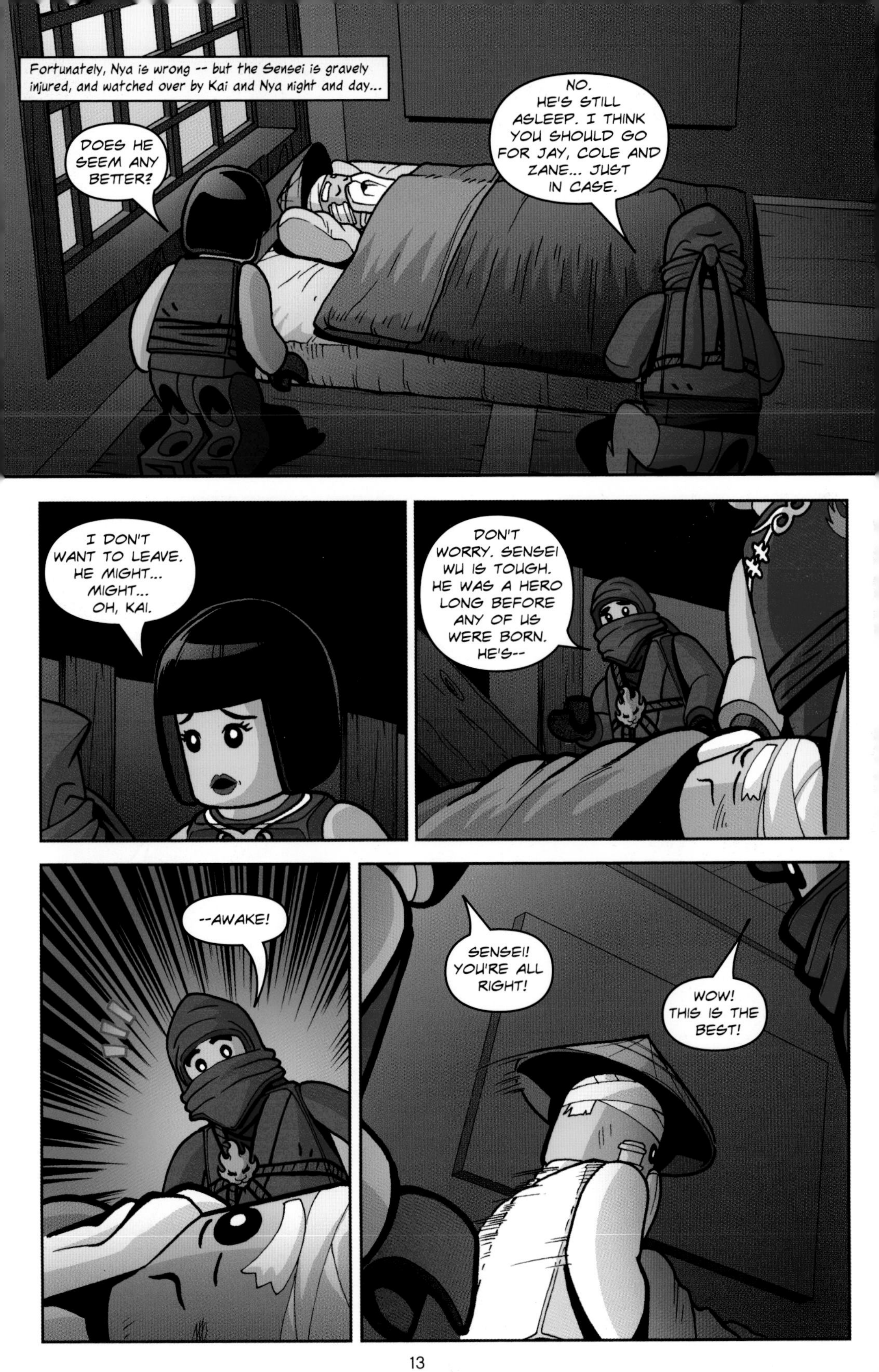
Fortunately, Nya is wrong -- but the Sensei is gravely injured, and watched over by Kai and Nya night and day...
DOES HE SEEM ANY BETTER?
NO. HE'S STILL ASLEEP. I THINK YOU SHOULD GO FOR JAY, COLE AND ZANE... JUST IN CASE.
I DON'T WANT TO LEAVE. HE MIGHT... MIGHT... OH, KAI.
DON'T WORRY. SENSEI WU IS TOUGH. HE WAS A HERO LONG BEFORE ANY OF US WERE BORN. HE'S--
--AWAKE!
SENSEI! YOU'RE ALL RIGHT!
WOW! THIS IS THE BEST!

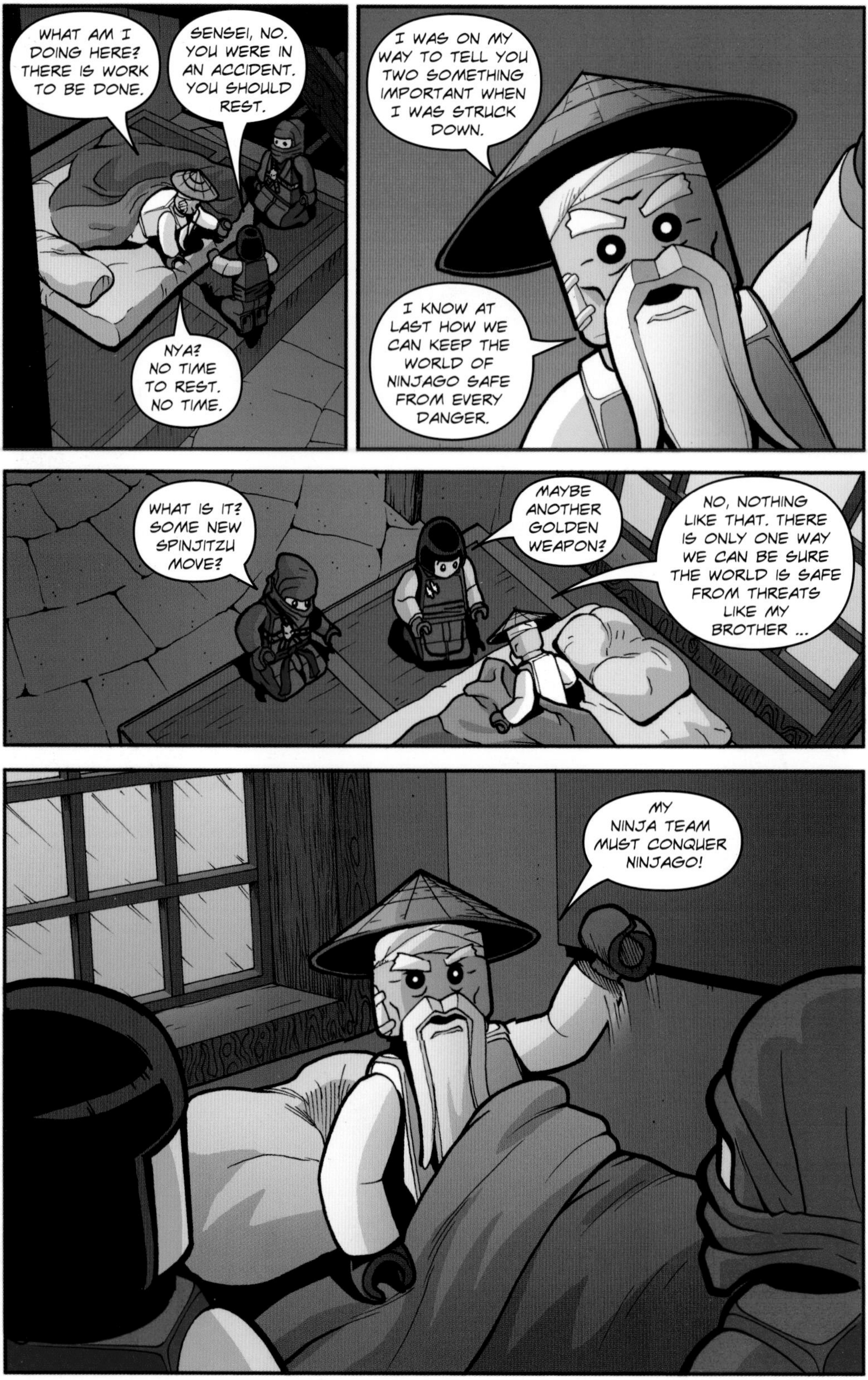
WHAT AM I DOING HERE? THERE IS WORK TO BE DONE.
SENSEI, NO. YOU WERE IN AN ACCIDENT. YOU SHOULD REST.
NYA? NO TIME TO REST. NO TIME.
I WAS ON MY WAY TO TELL YOU TWO SOMETHING IMPORTANT WHEN I WAS STRUCK DOWN.
I KNOW AT LAST HOW WE CAN KEEP THE WORLD OF NINJAGO SAFE FROM EVERY DANGER.
WHAT IS IT? SOME NEW SPINJITZU MOVE?
MAYBE ANOTHER GOLDEN WEAPON?
NO, NOTHING LIKE THAT. THERE IS ONLY ONE WAY WE CAN BE SURE THE WORLD IS SAFE FROM THREATS LIKE MY BROTHER ...
MY NINJA TEAM MUST CONQUER NINJAGO!

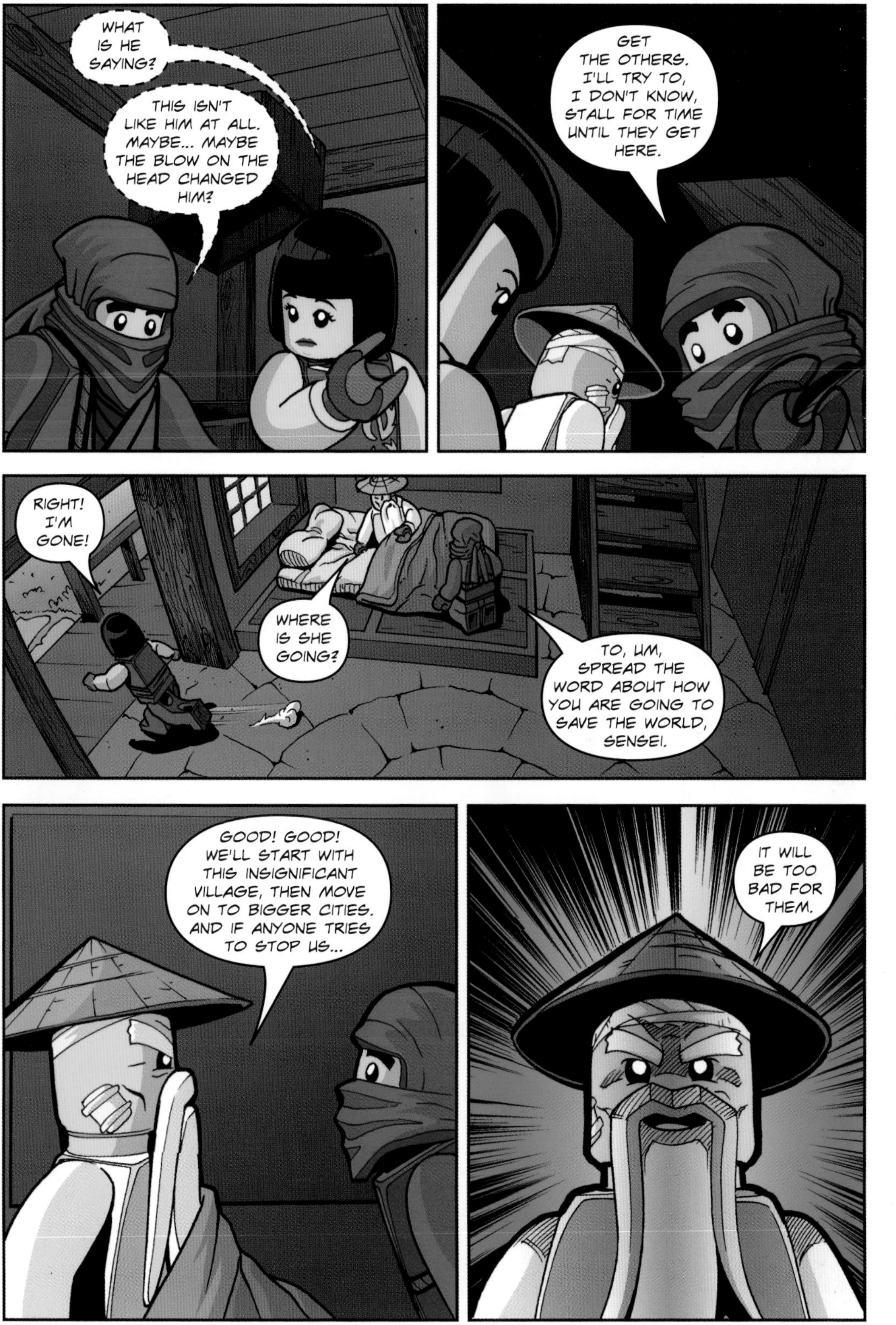
WHAT IS HE SAYING?
THIS ISN'T LIKE HIM AT ALL. MAYBE... MAYBE THE BLOW ON THE HEAD CHANGED HIM?
GET THE OTHERS. I'LL TRY TO, I DON'T KNOW, STALL FOR TIME UNTIL THEY GET HERE.
RIGHT! I'M GONE!
WHERE IS SHE GOING?
TO, UM, SPREAD THE WORD ABOUT HOW YOU ARE GOING TO SAVE THE WORLD, SENSEI.
GOOD! GOOD! WE'LL START WITH THIS INSIGNIFICANT VILLAGE, THEN MOVE ON TO BIGGER CITIES. AND IF ANYONE TRIES TO STOP US...
IT WILL BE TOO BAD FOR THEM.

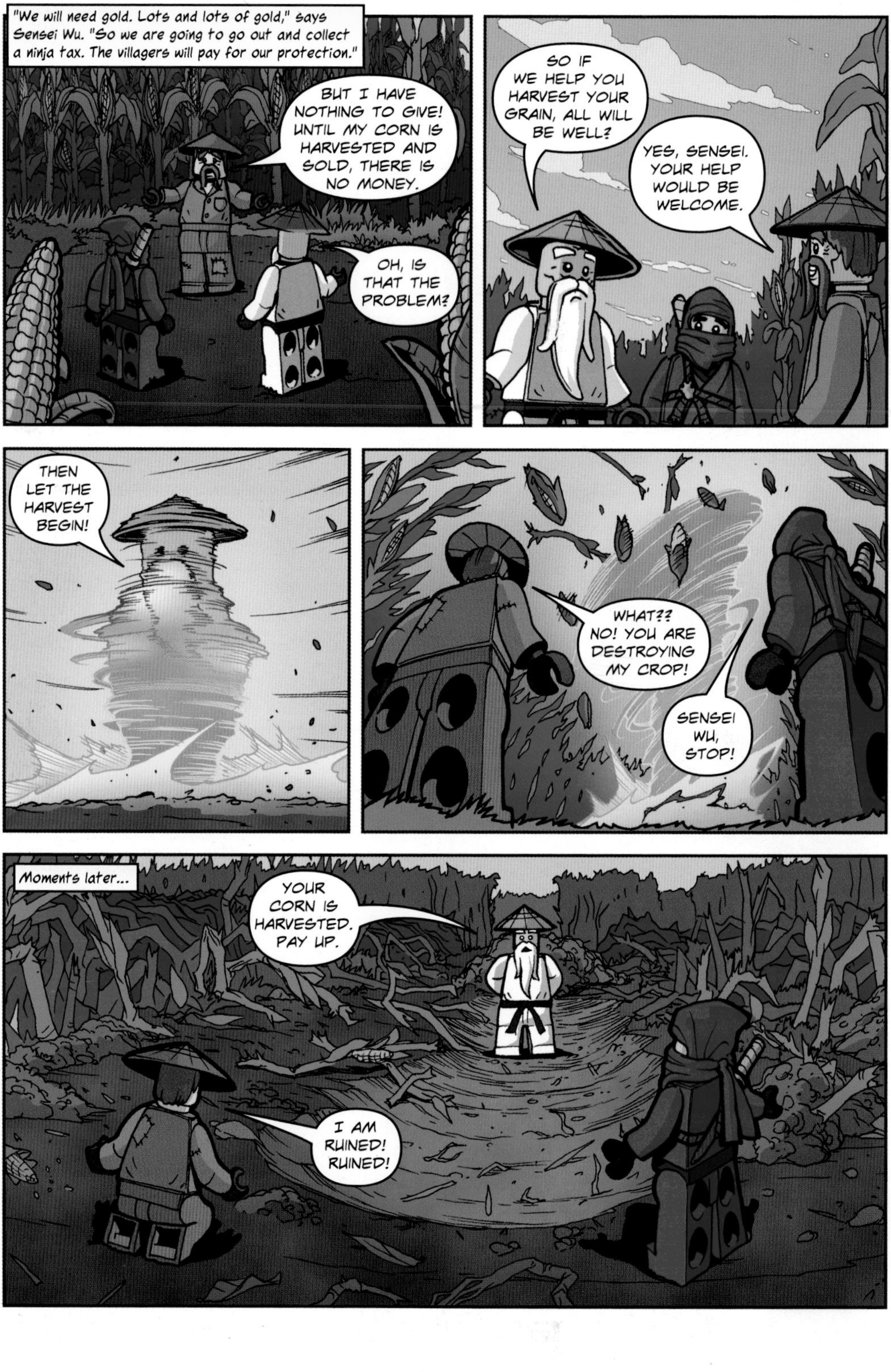
"We will need gold. Lots and lots of gold," says Sensei Wu. "So we are going to go out and collect a ninja tax. The villagers will pay for our protection."
BUT I HAVE NOTHING TO GIVE! UNTIL MY CORN IS HARVESTED AND SOLD, THERE IS NO MONEY.
OH, IS THAT THE PROBLEM?
SO IF WE HELP YOU HARVEST YOUR GRAIN, ALL WILL BE WELL?
YES, SENSEI. YOUR HELP WOULD BE WELCOME.
THEN LET THE HARVEST BEGIN!
WHAT?? NO! YOU ARE DESTROYING MY CROP!
SENSEI WU, STOP!
Moments later...
YOUR CORN IS HARVESTED. PAY UP.
I AM RUINED! RUINED!

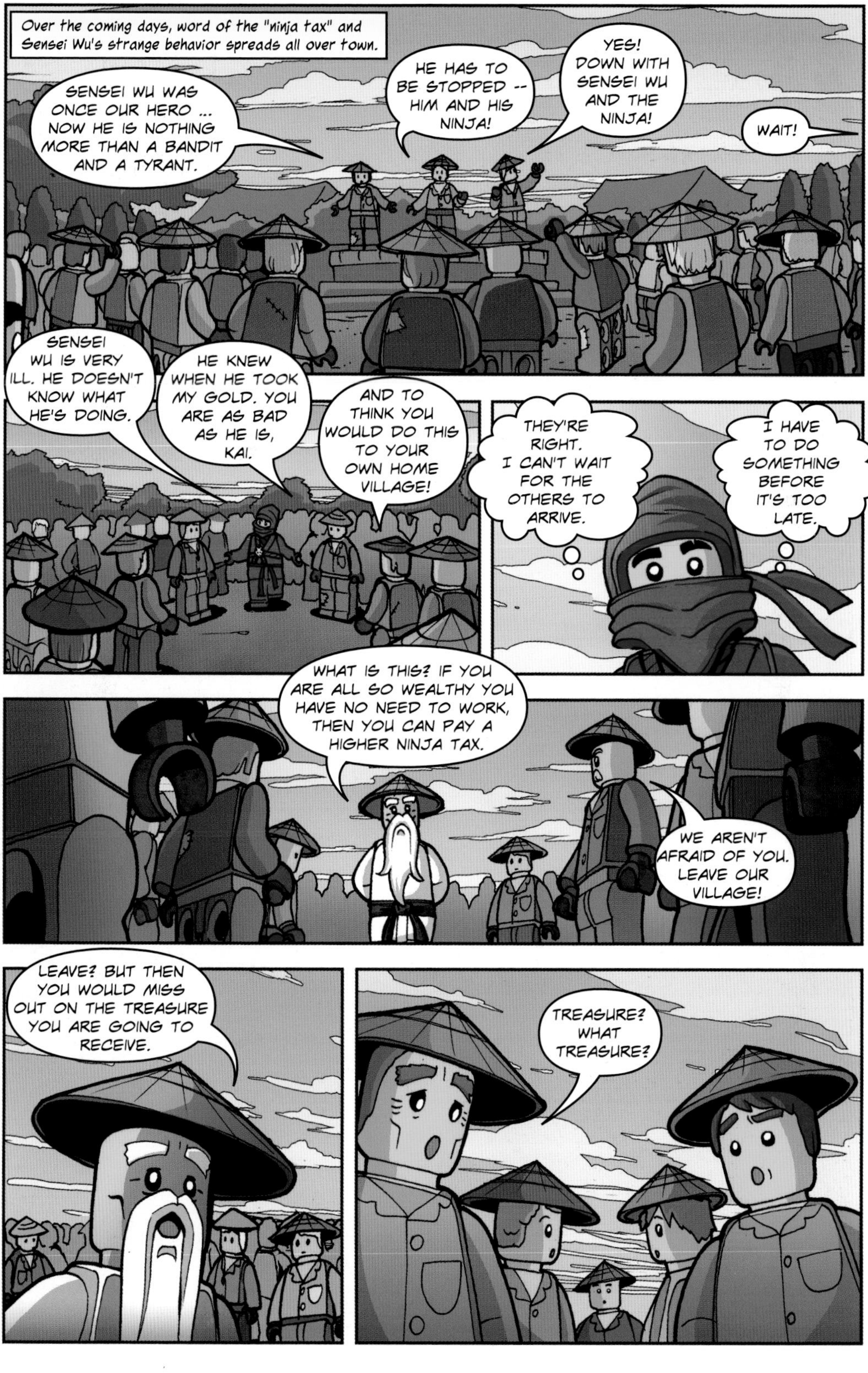
Over the coming days, word of the "ninja tax" and Sensei Wu's strange behavior spreads all over town.
SENSEI WU WAS ONCE OUR HERO ... NOW HE IS NOTHING MORE THAN A BANDIT AND A TYRANT.
HE HAS TO BE STOPPED -- HIM AND HIS NINJA!
YES! DOWN WITH SENSEI WU AND THE NINJA!
WAIT!
SENSEI WU IS VERY ILL. HE DOESN'T KNOW WHAT HE'S DOING.
HE KNEW WHEN HE TOOK MY GOLD. YOU ARE AS BAD AS HE IS, KAI.
AND TO THINK YOU WOULD DO THIS TO YOUR OWN HOME VILLAGE!
THEY'RE RIGHT. I CAN'T WAIT FOR THE OTHERS TO ARRIVE.
I HAVE TO DO SOMETHING BEFORE IT'S TOO LATE.
WHAT IS THIS? IF YOU ARE ALL SO WEALTHY YOU HAVE NO NEED TO WORK, THEN YOU CAN PAY A HIGHER NINJA TAX.
WE AREN'T AFRAID OF YOU. LEAVE OUR VILLAGE!
LEAVE? BUT THEN YOU WOULD MISS OUT ON THE TREASURE YOU ARE GOING TO RECEIVE.
TREASURE? WHAT TREASURE?

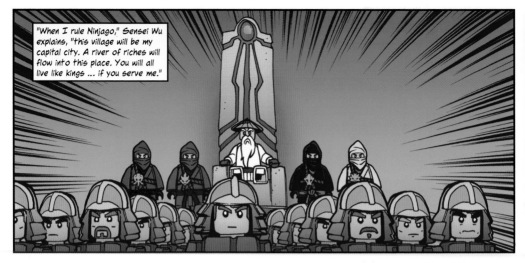

"When I rule Ninjago," Sensei Wu explains, "this village will be my capital city. A river of riches will flow into this place. You will all live like kings ... if you serve me."

KINGS, HUH? I LIKE THE SOUND OF THAT!

SENSEI WU HAS ALWAYS KNOWN WHAT IS BEST, RIGHT?

HOORAY FOR SENSEI WU!

DID YOU MEAN ALL THAT, ABOUT THE VILLAGE BEING YOUR CAPITAL ONE DAY?

THIS VILLAGE IS GOING TO BE VERY IMPORTANT, KAI.

WHEN MY OTHER NINJA GET HERE -- YES, I KNOW THEY ARE COMING -- THE FOUR OF YOU ARE GOING TO DESTROY THIS SANDPIT.

THEN NO ONE WILL DARE TO GET IN MY WAY AGAIN.

I CAN'T LET YOU DO THIS, SENSEI! YOU'RE ILL...

YOU'RE NOT YOURSELF. AND THIS HAS TO STOP, NOW ... EVEN IF I HAVE TO BE THE ONE TO STOP YOU.

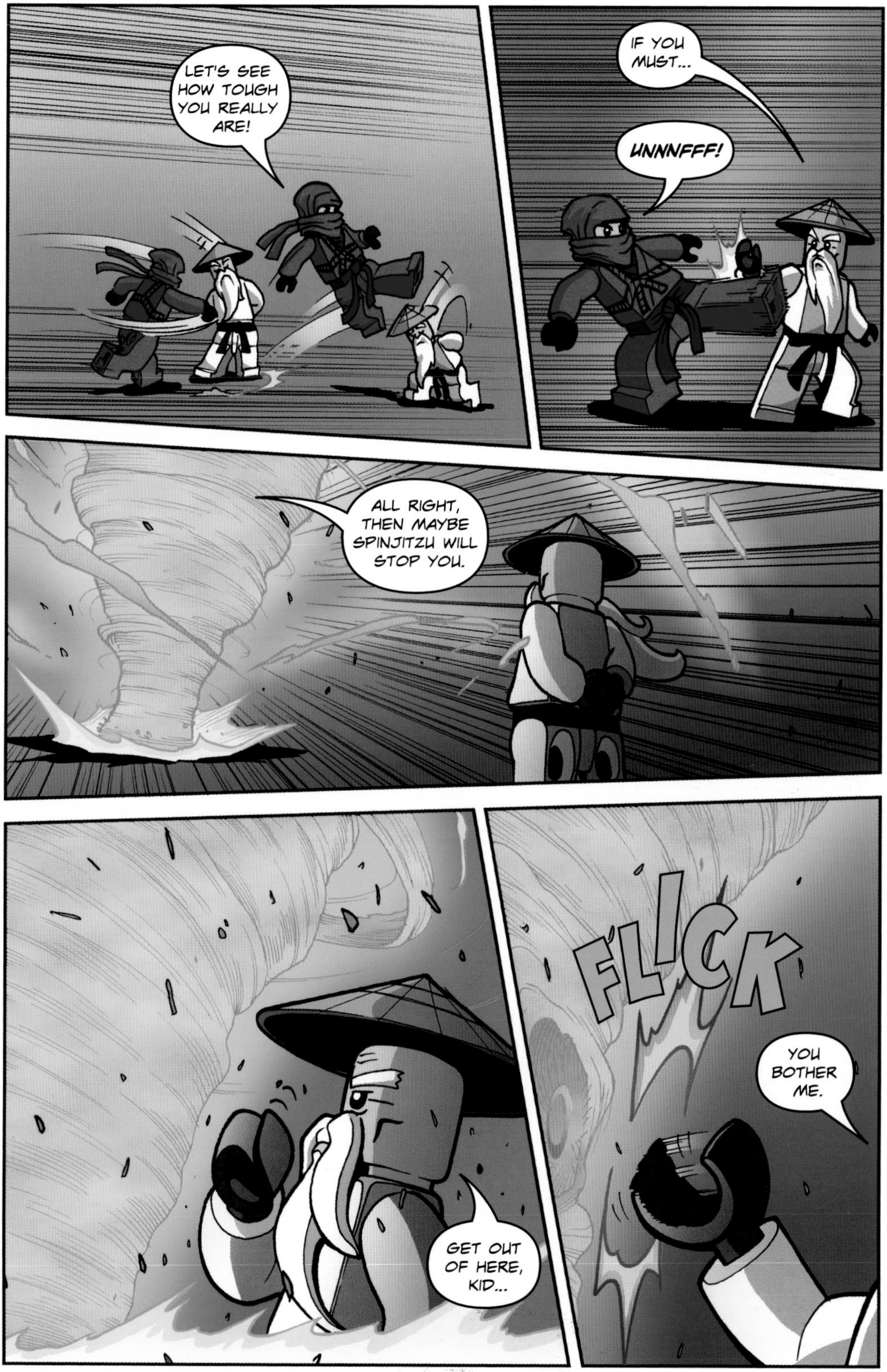
LET'S SEE HOW TOUGH YOU REALLY ARE!
IF YOU MUST...
UNNNFFF!
ALL RIGHT, THEN MAYBE SPINJITZU WILL STOP YOU.
GET OUT OF HERE, KID...
FLICK
YOU BOTHER ME.

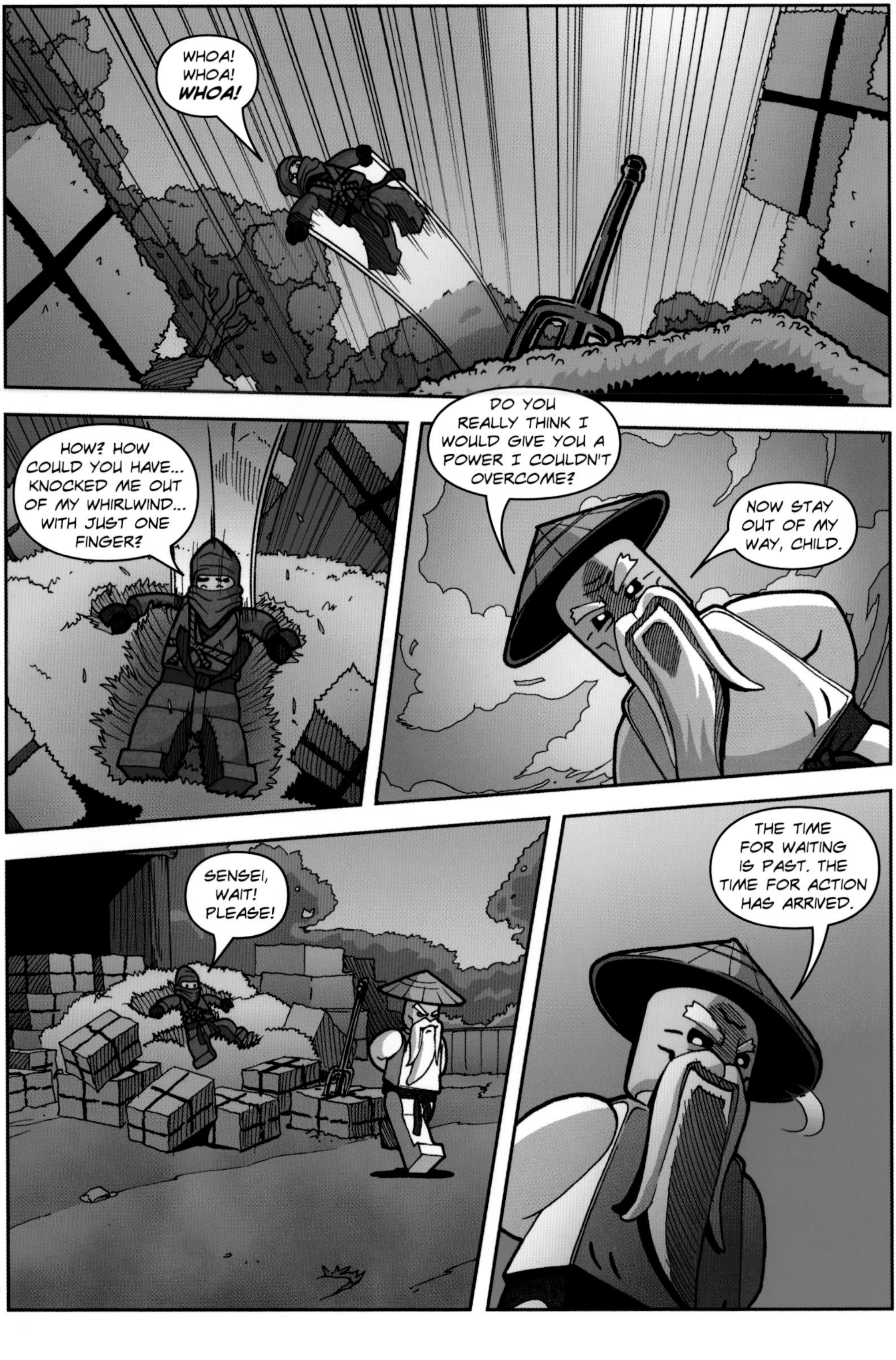
WHOA! WHOA! WHOA!
HOW? HOW COULD YOU HAVE... KNOCKED ME OUT OF MY WHIRLWIND... WITH JUST ONE FINGER?
DO YOU REALLY THINK I WOULD GIVE YOU A POWER I COULDN'T OVERCOME?
NOW STAY OUT OF MY WAY, CHILD.
SENSEI, WAIT! PLEASE!
THE TIME FOR WAITING IS PAST. THE TIME FOR ACTION HAS ARRIVED.

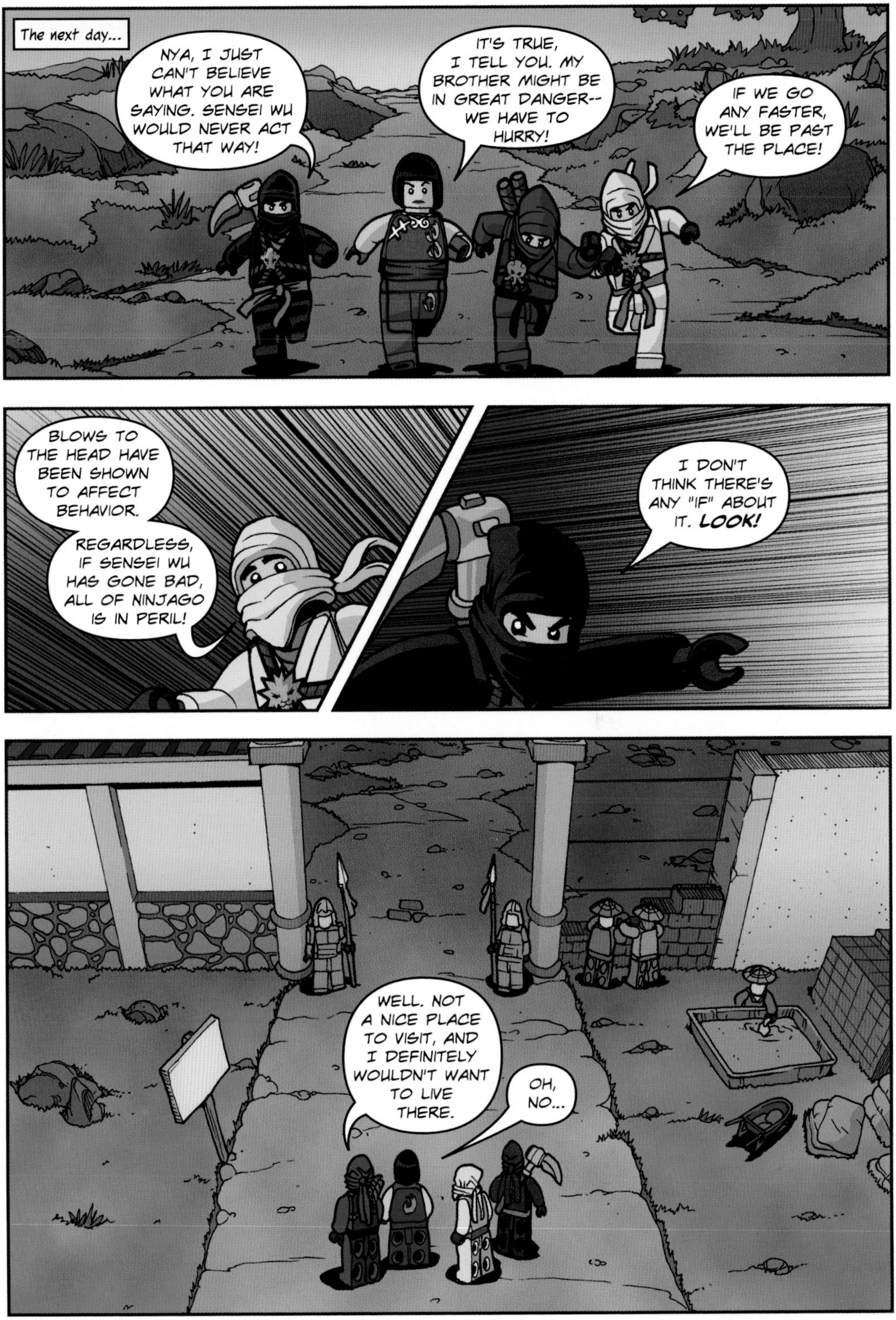
The next day...
NYA, I JUST CAN'T BELIEVE WHAT YOU ARE SAYING. SENSEI WU WOULD NEVER ACT THAT WAY!
IT'S TRUE, I TELL YOU. MY BROTHER MIGHT BE IN GREAT DANGER-- WE HAVE TO HURRY!
IF WE GO ANY FASTER, WE'LL BE PAST THE PLACE!
BLOWS TO THE HEAD HAVE BEEN SHOWN TO AFFECT BEHAVIOR.
REGARDLESS, IF SENSEI WU HAS GONE BAD, ALL OF NINJAGO IS IN PERIL!
I DON'T THINK THERE'S ANY "IF" ABOUT IT. LOOK!
WELL. NOT A NICE PLACE TO VISIT, AND I DEFINITELY WOULDN'T WANT TO LIVE THERE.
OH, NO...

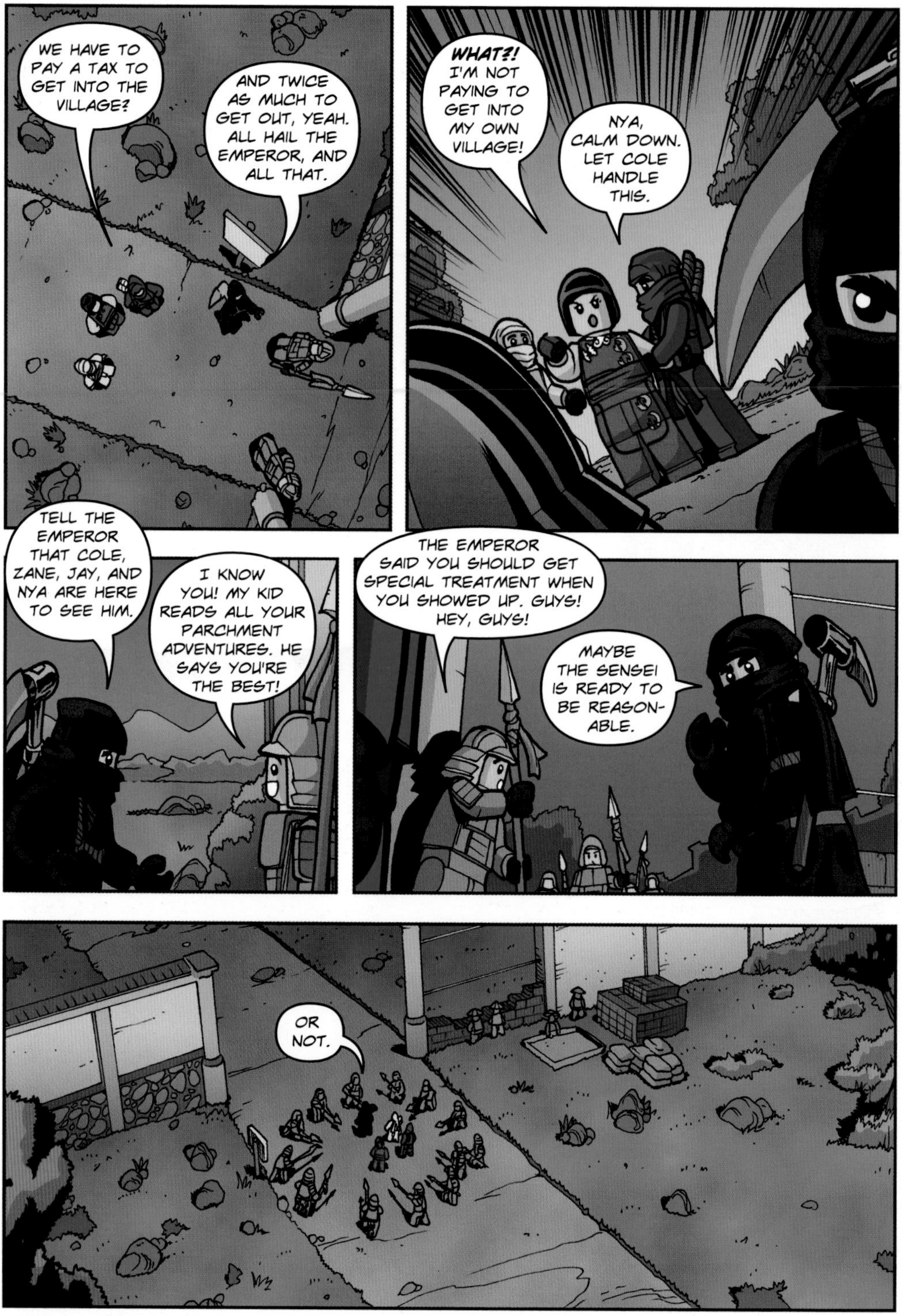
WE HAVE TO PAY A TAX TO GET INTO THE VILLAGE?
AND TWICE AS MUCH TO GET OUT, YEAH. ALL HAIL THE EMPEROR, AND ALL THAT.
WHAT?! I'M NOT PAYING TO GET INTO MY OWN VILLAGE!
NYA, CALM DOWN. LET COLE HANDLE THIS.
TELL THE EMPEROR THAT COLE, ZANE, JAY, AND NYA ARE HERE TO SEE HIM.
I KNOW YOU! MY KID READS ALL YOUR PARCHMENT ADVENTURES. HE SAYS YOU'RE THE BEST!
THE EMPEROR SAID YOU SHOULD GET SPECIAL TREATMENT WHEN YOU SHOWED UP. GUYS! HEY, GUYS!
MAYBE THE SENSEI IS READY TO BE REASON-ABLE.
OR NOT.

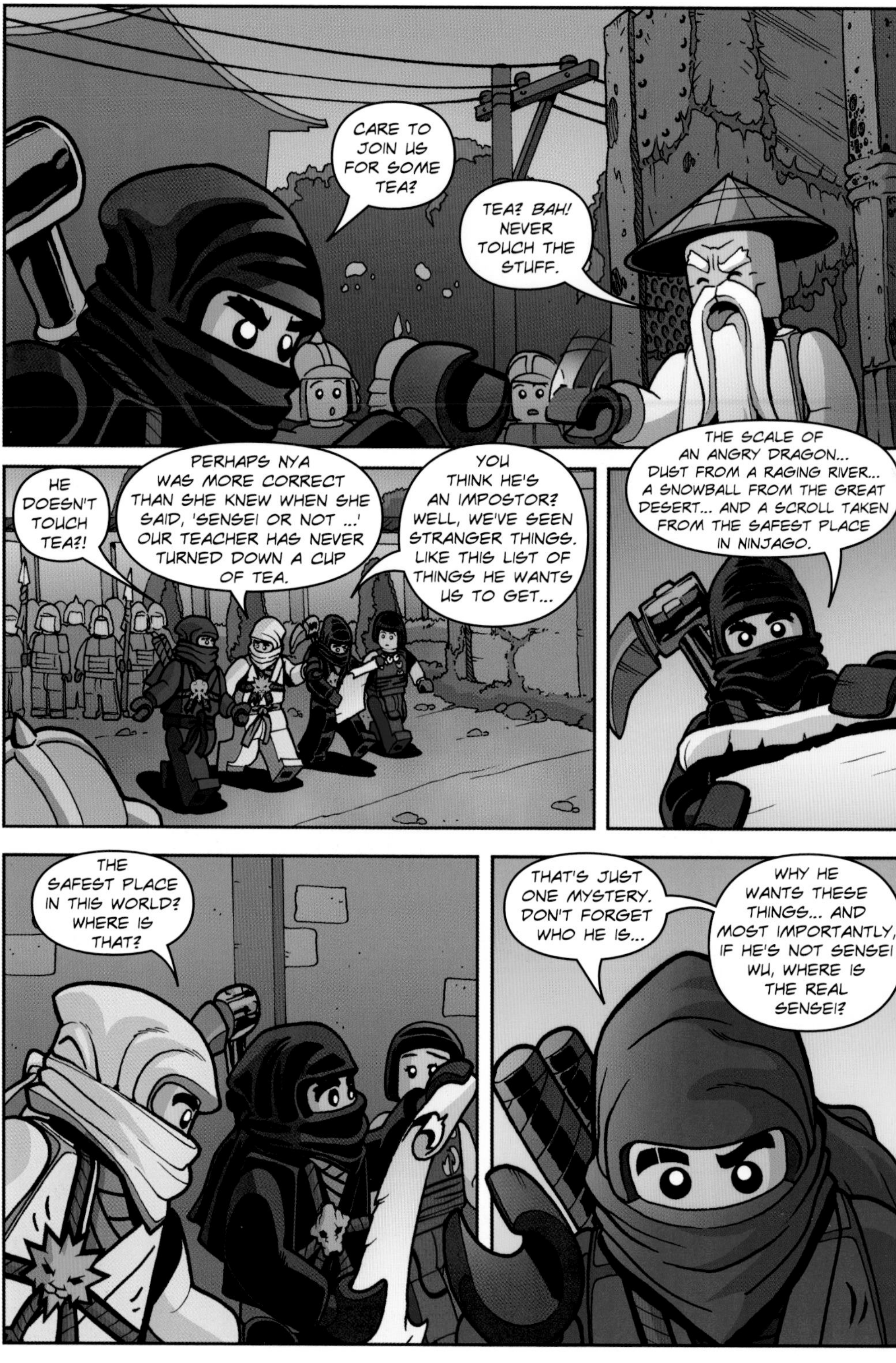
CARE TO JOIN US FOR SOME TEA?
TEA? BAH! NEVER TOUCH THE STUFF.
HE DOESN'T TOUCH TEA?!
PERHAPS NYA WAS MORE CORRECT THAN SHE KNEW WHEN SHE SAID, 'SENSEI OR NOT ...' OUR TEACHER HAS NEVER TURNED DOWN A CUP OF TEA.
YOU THINK HE'S AN IMPOSTOR? WELL, WE'VE SEEN STRANGER THINGS. LIKE THIS LIST OF THINGS HE WANTS US TO GET...
THE SCALE OF AN ANGRY DRAGON... DUST FROM A RAGING RIVER... A SNOWBALL FROM THE GREAT DESERT... AND A SCROLL TAKEN FROM THE SAFEST PLACE IN NINJAGO.
THE SAFEST PLACE IN THIS WORLD? WHERE IS THAT?
THAT'S JUST ONE MYSTERY. DON'T FORGET WHO HE IS...
WHY HE WANTS THESE THINGS... AND MOST IMPORTANTLY, IF HE'S NOT SENSEI WU, WHERE IS THE REAL SENSEI?

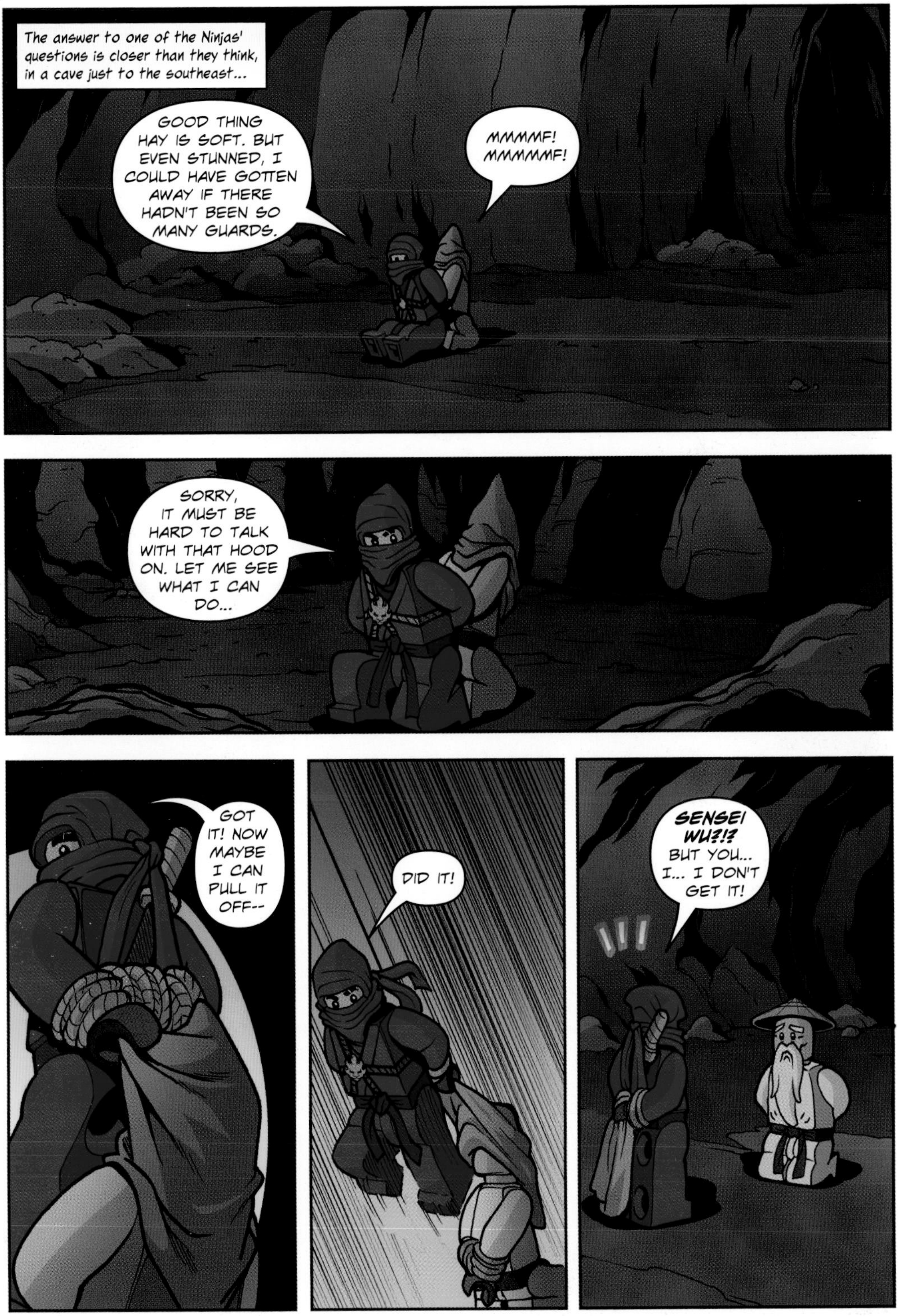
The answer to one of the Ninjas' questions is closer than they think, in a cave just to the southeast...
GOOD THING HAY IS SOFT. BUT EVEN STUNNED, I COULD HAVE GOTTEN AWAY IF THERE HADN'T BEEN SO MANY GUARDS.
MMMMF! MMMMMF!
SORRY, IT MUST BE HARD TO TALK WITH THAT HOOD ON. LET ME SEE WHAT I CAN DO...
GOT IT! NOW MAYBE I CAN PULL IT OFF--
DID IT!
SENSEI WU?!? BUT YOU... I... I DON'T GET IT!

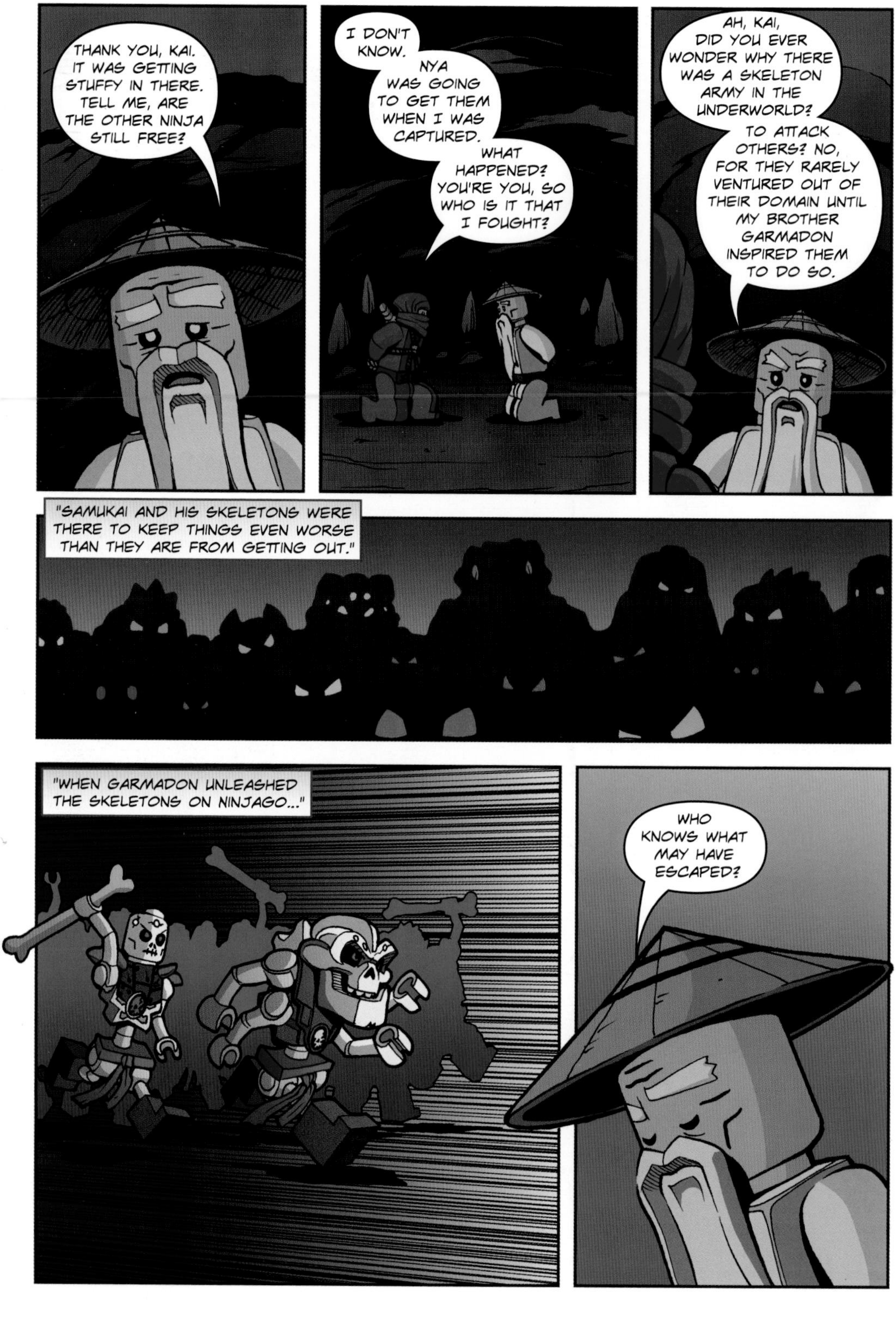
THANK YOU, KAI. IT WAS GETTING STUFFY IN THERE. TELL ME, ARE THE OTHER NINJA STILL FREE?
I DON'T KNOW.
NYA WAS GOING TO GET THEM WHEN I WAS CAPTURED.
WHAT HAPPENED? YOU'RE YOU, SO WHO IS IT THAT I FOUGHT?
AH, KAI, DID YOU EVER WONDER WHY THERE WAS A SKELETON ARMY IN THE UNDERWORLD?
TO ATTACK OTHERS? NO, FOR THEY RARELY VENTURED OUT OF THEIR DOMAIN UNTIL MY BROTHER GARMADON INSPIRED THEM TO DO SO.
"SAMUKAI AND HIS SKELETONS WERE THERE TO KEEP THINGS EVEN WORSE THAN THEY ARE FROM GETTING OUT."
"WHEN GARMADON UNLEASHED THE SKELETONS ON NINJAGO..."
WHO KNOWS WHAT MAY HAVE ESCAPED?

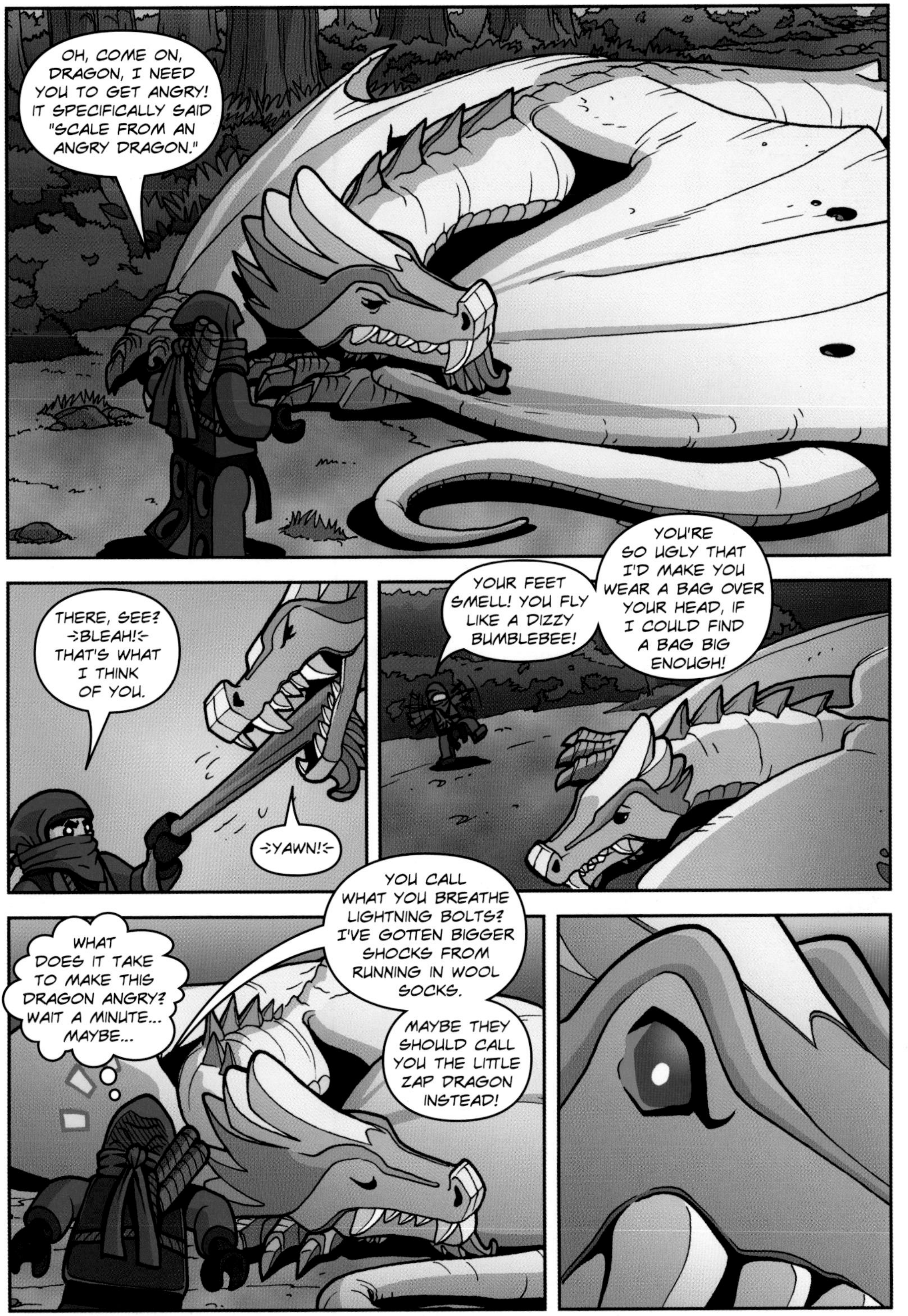

OH, COME ON, DRAGON, I NEED YOU TO GET ANGRY! IT SPECIFICALLY SAID "SCALE FROM AN ANGRY DRAGON."
THERE, SEE? -BLEAH!- THAT'S WHAT I THINK OF YOU.
-YAWN!-
YOUR FEET SMELL! YOU FLY LIKE A DIZZY BUMBLEBEE!
YOU'RE SO UGLY THAT I'D MAKE YOU WEAR A BAG OVER YOUR HEAD, IF I COULD FIND A BAG BIG ENOUGH!
WHAT DOES IT TAKE TO MAKE THIS DRAGON ANGRY? WAIT A MINUTE... MAYBE...
YOU CALL WHAT YOU BREATHE LIGHTNING BOLTS? I'VE GOTTEN BIGGER SHOCKS FROM RUNNING IN WOOL SOCKS.
MAYBE THEY SHOULD CALL YOU THE LITTLE ZAP DRAGON INSTEAD!

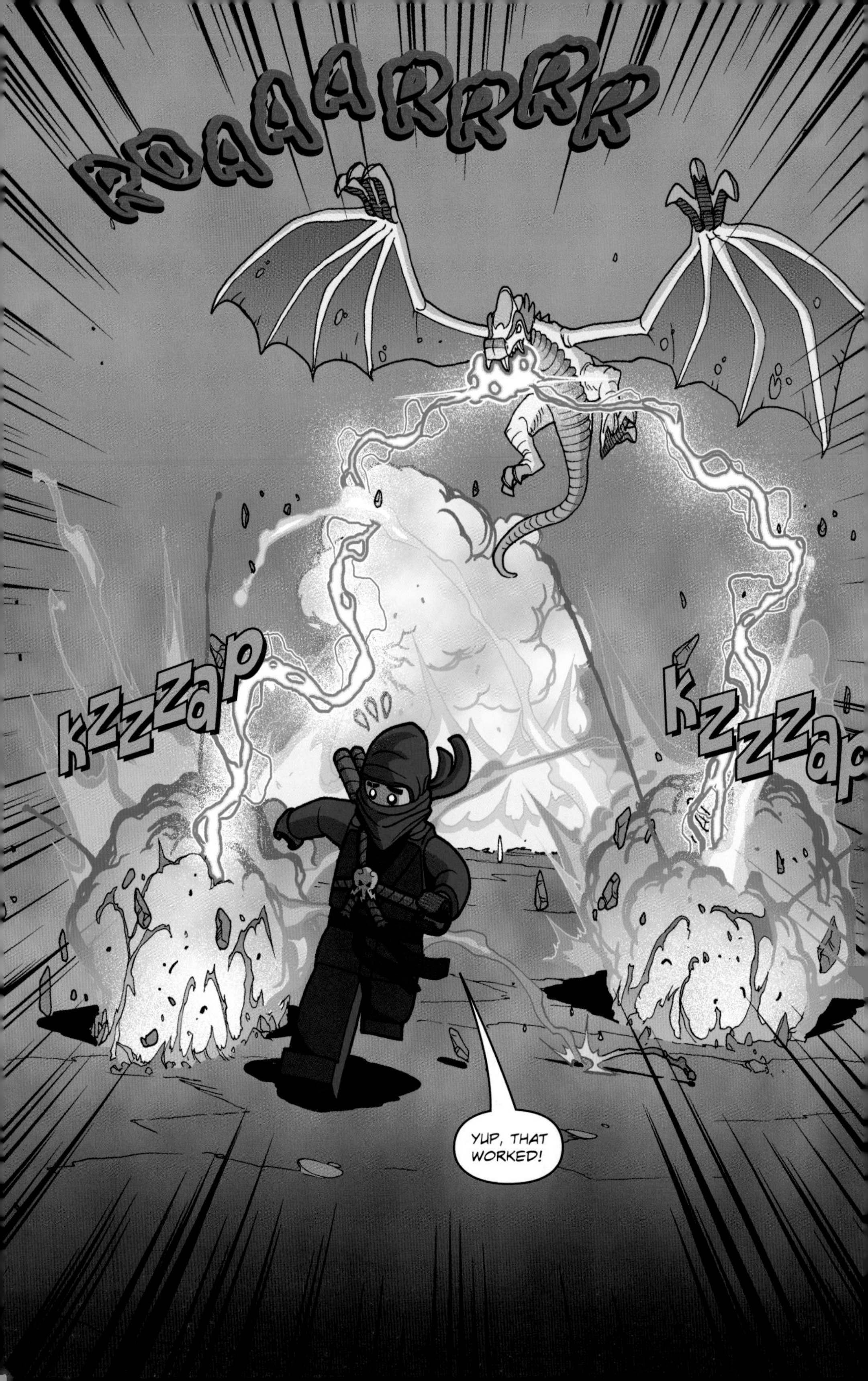
ROOAAARRRRR
KZZZAP
KZZZAP
YUP, THAT WORKED!

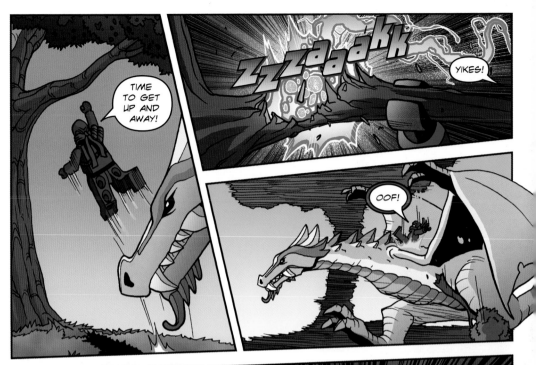

TIME TO GET UP AND AWAY!

YIKES!

OOF!

THIS SHOULD DO IT.

ONE SCALE FROM AN ANGRY DRAGON... PIECE OF CAKE!

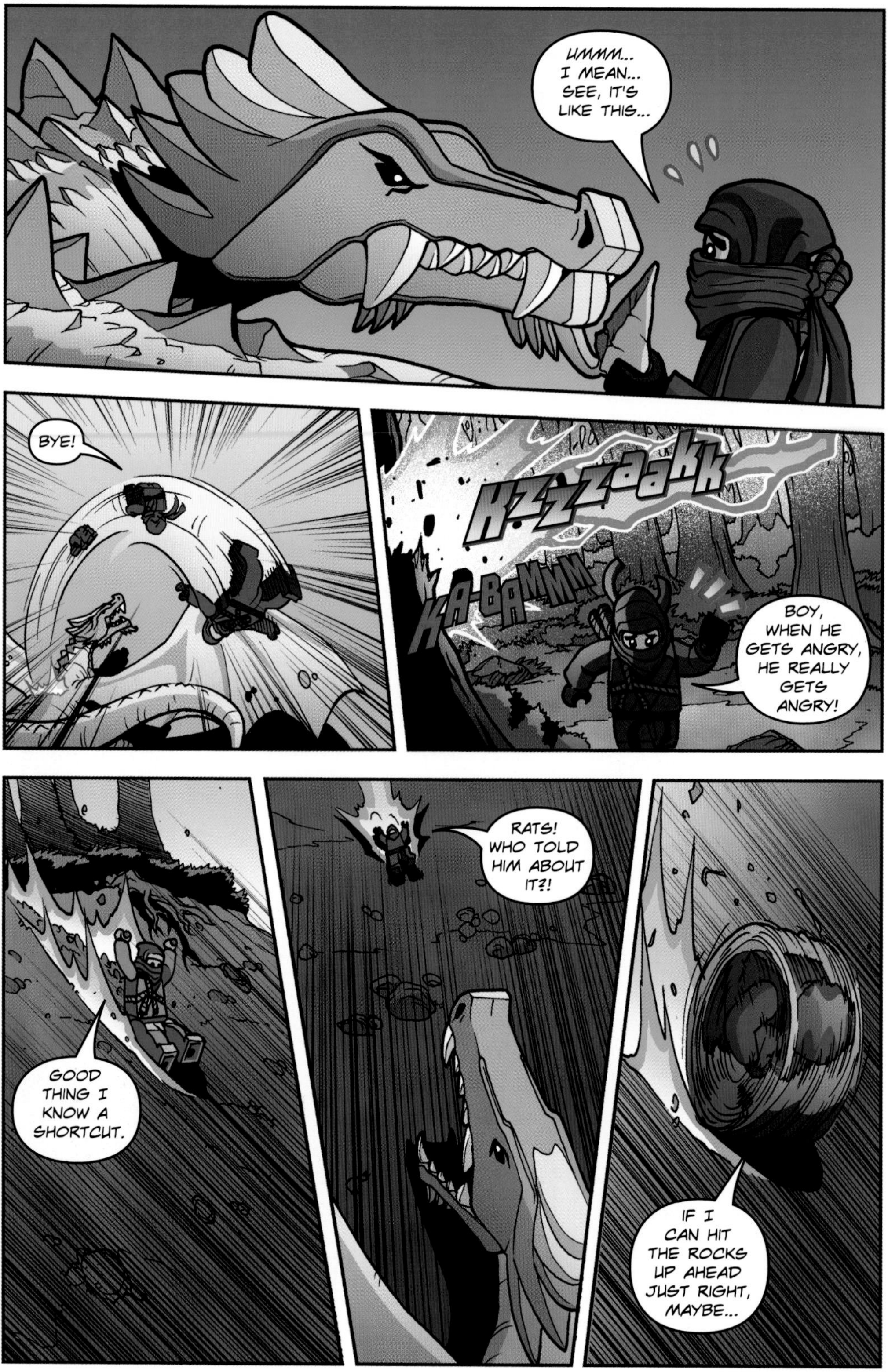

UMMM... I MEAN... SEE, IT'S LIKE THIS...
BYE!
KZZZAAKK
KA-BAMMM
BOY, WHEN HE GETS ANGRY, HE REALLY GETS ANGRY!
GOOD THING I KNOW A SHORTCUT.
RATS! WHO TOLD HIM ABOUT IT?!
IF I CAN HIT THE ROCKS UP AHEAD JUST RIGHT, MAYBE...

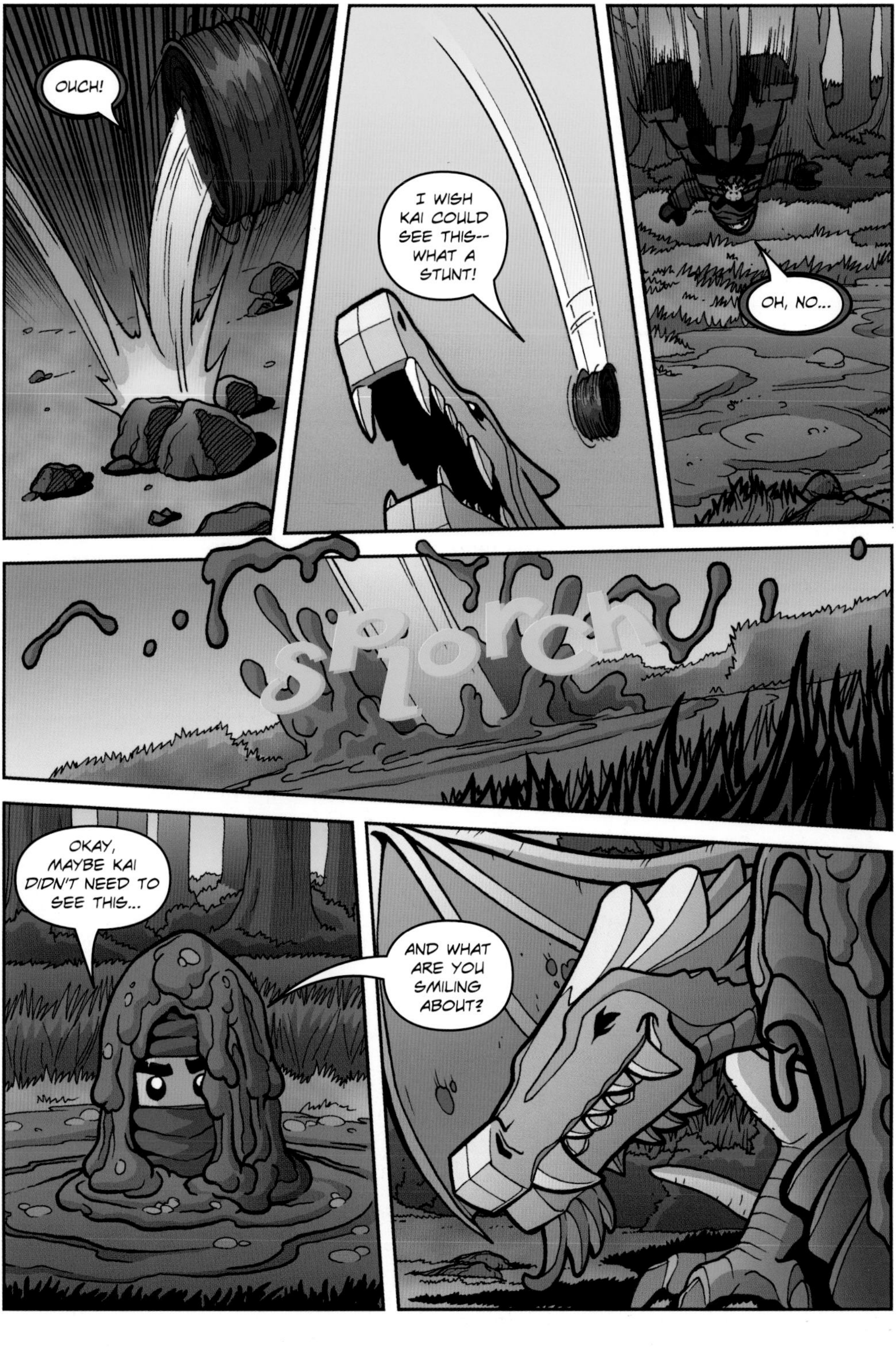
OUCH!
I WISH KAI COULD SEE THIS-- WHAT A STUNT!
OH, NO...
SPLORCH
OKAY, MAYBE KAI DIDN'T NEED TO SEE THIS...
AND WHAT ARE YOU SMILING ABOUT?

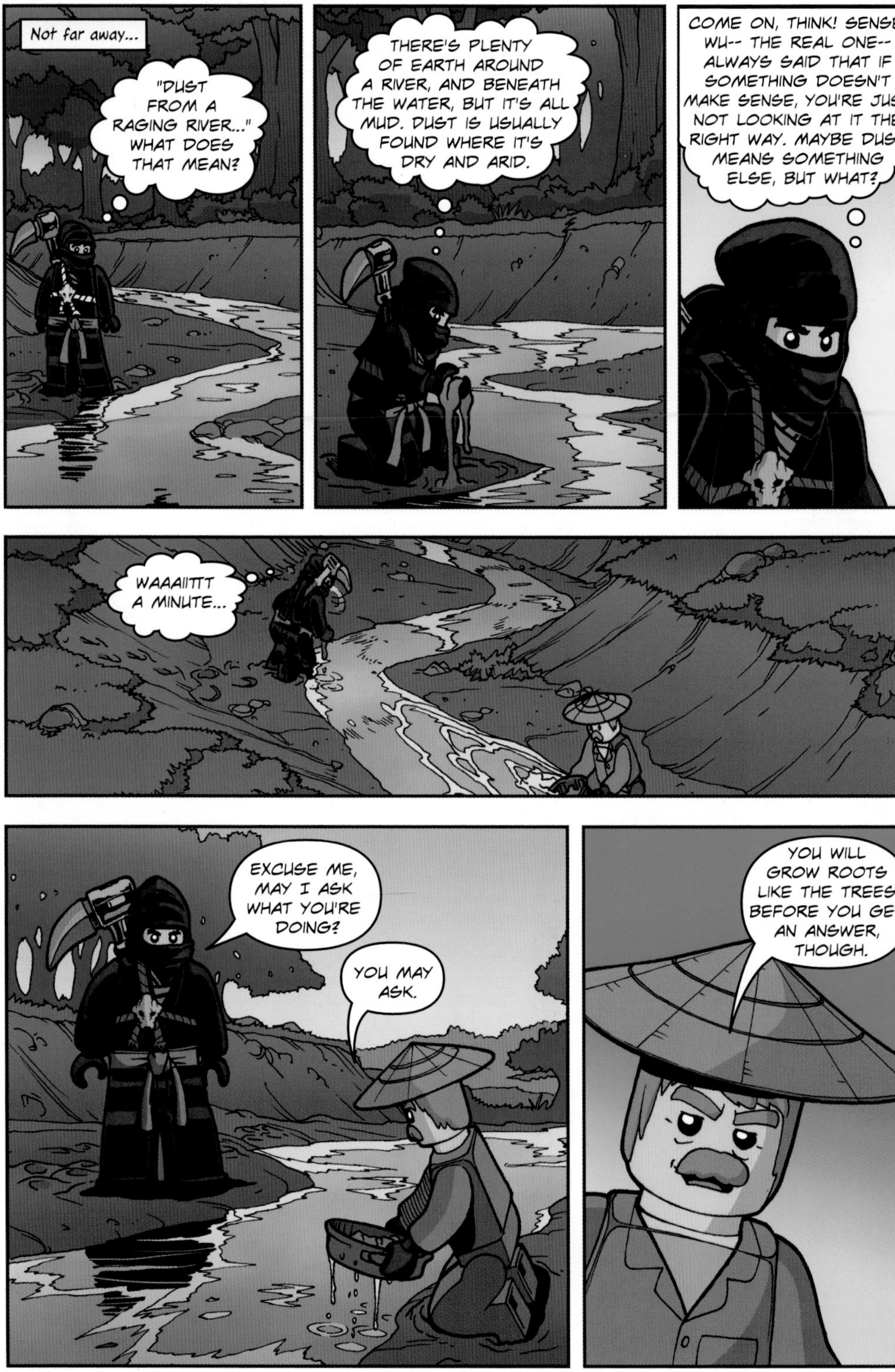
Not far away...
"DUST FROM A RAGING RIVER..." WHAT DOES THAT MEAN?
THERE'S PLENTY OF EARTH AROUND A RIVER, AND BENEATH THE WATER, BUT IT'S ALL MUD. DUST IS USUALLY FOUND WHERE IT'S DRY AND ARID.
COME ON, THINK! SENSEI WU-- THE REAL ONE-- ALWAYS SAID THAT IF SOMETHING DOESN'T MAKE SENSE, YOU'RE JUST NOT LOOKING AT IT THE RIGHT WAY. MAYBE DUST MEANS SOMETHING ELSE, BUT WHAT?
WAAAIITTT A MINUTE...
EXCUSE ME, MAY I ASK WHAT YOU'RE DOING?
YOU MAY ASK.
YOU WILL GROW ROOTS LIKE THE TREES BEFORE YOU GET AN ANSWER, THOUGH.

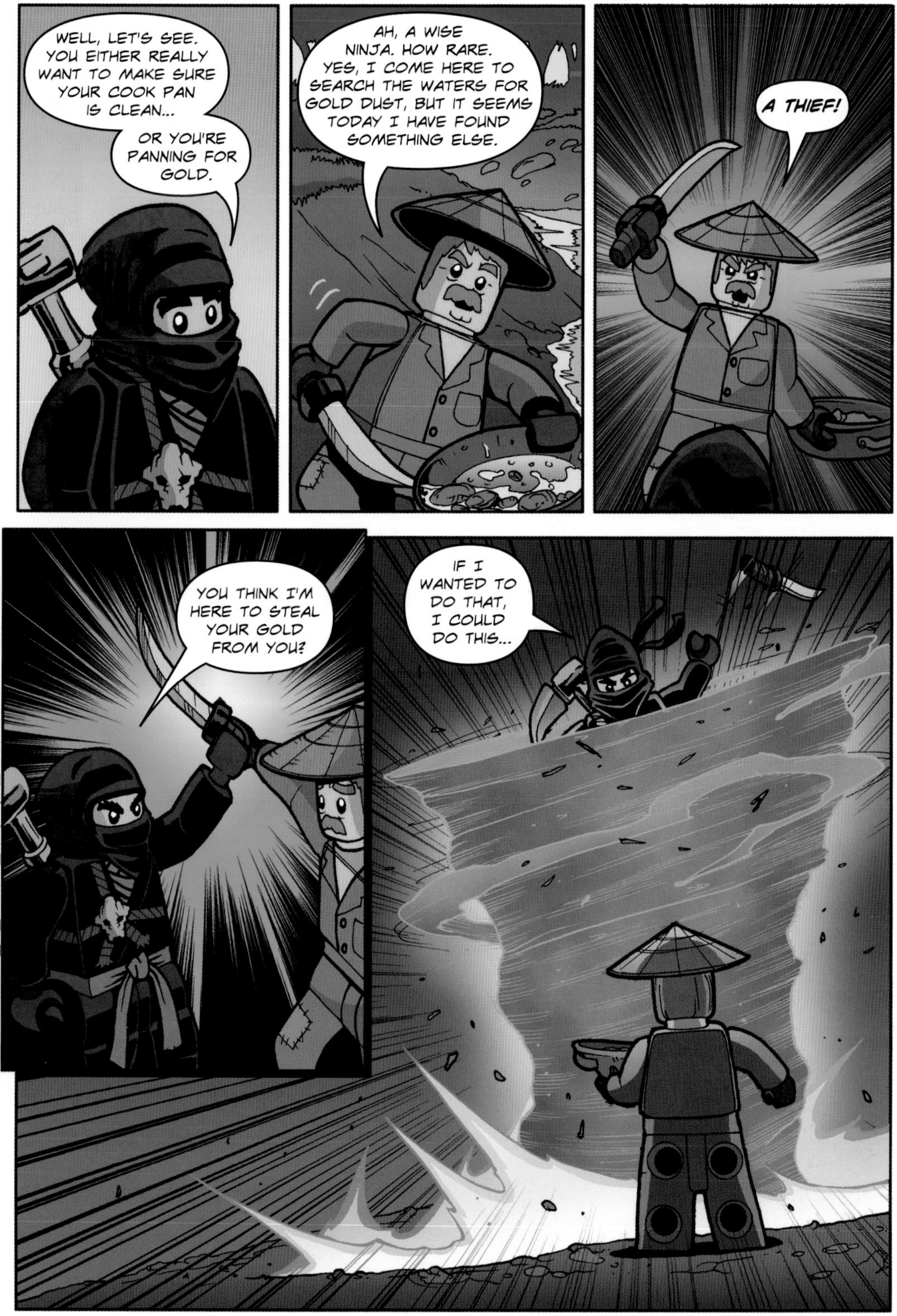
WELL, LET'S SEE. YOU EITHER REALLY WANT TO MAKE SURE YOUR COOK PAN IS CLEAN...
OR YOU'RE PANNING FOR GOLD.
AH, A WISE NINJA. HOW RARE. YES, I COME HERE TO SEARCH THE WATERS FOR GOLD DUST, BUT IT SEEMS TODAY I HAVE FOUND SOMETHING ELSE.
A THIEF!
YOU THINK I'M HERE TO STEAL YOUR GOLD FROM YOU?
IF I WANTED TO DO THAT, I COULD DO THIS...

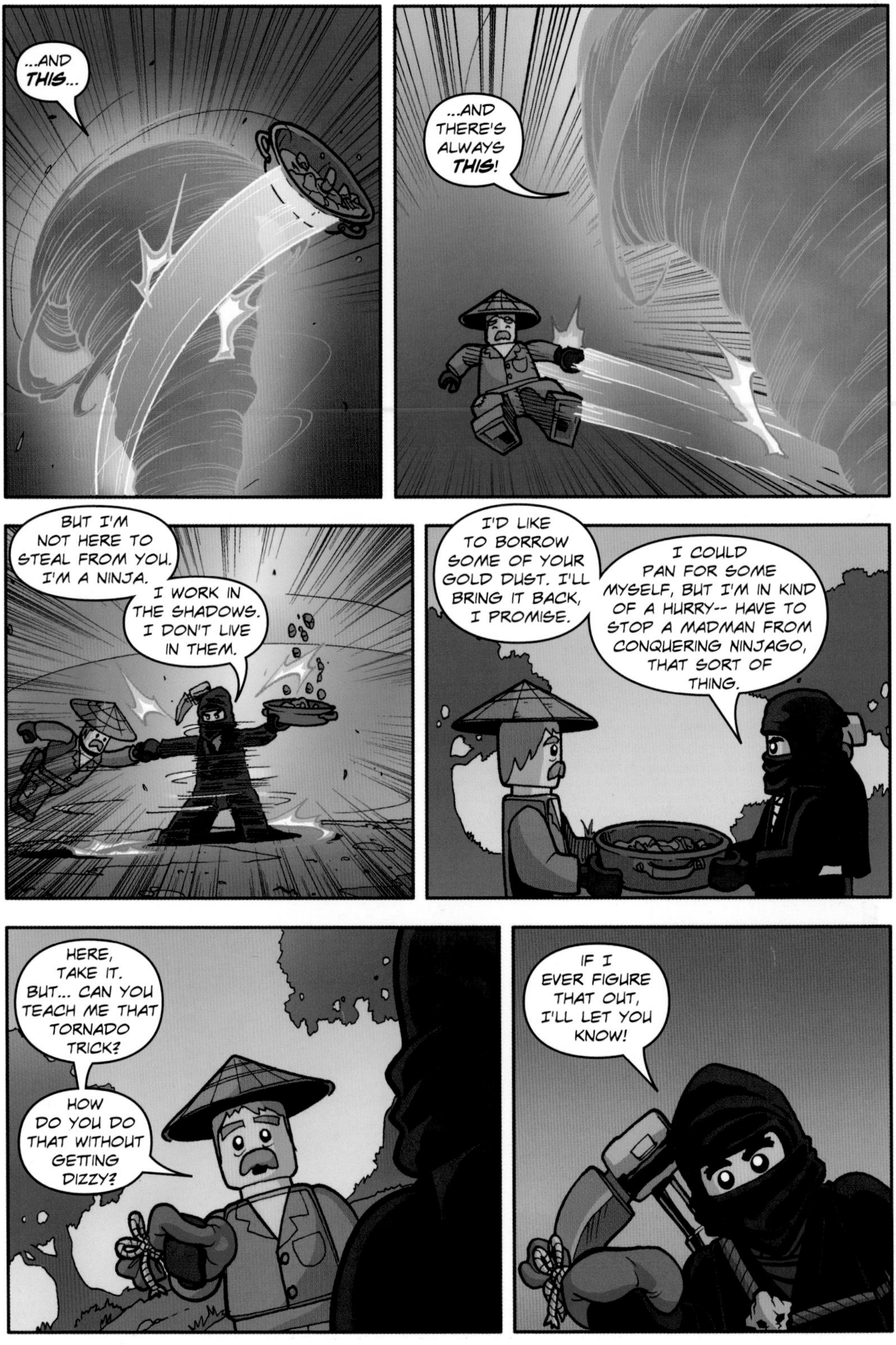
...AND THIS...
...AND THERE'S ALWAYS THIS!
BUT I'M NOT HERE TO STEAL FROM YOU. I'M A NINJA.
I WORK IN THE SHADOWS. I DON'T LIVE IN THEM.
I'D LIKE TO BORROW SOME OF YOUR GOLD DUST. I'LL BRING IT BACK, I PROMISE.
I COULD PAN FOR SOME MYSELF, BUT I'M IN KIND OF A HURRY-- HAVE TO STOP A MADMAN FROM CONQUERING NINJAGO, THAT SORT OF THING.
HERE, TAKE IT. BUT... CAN YOU TEACH ME THAT TORNADO TRICK?
HOW DO YOU DO THAT WITHOUT GETTING DIZZY?
IF I EVER FIGURE THAT OUT, I'LL LET YOU KNOW!

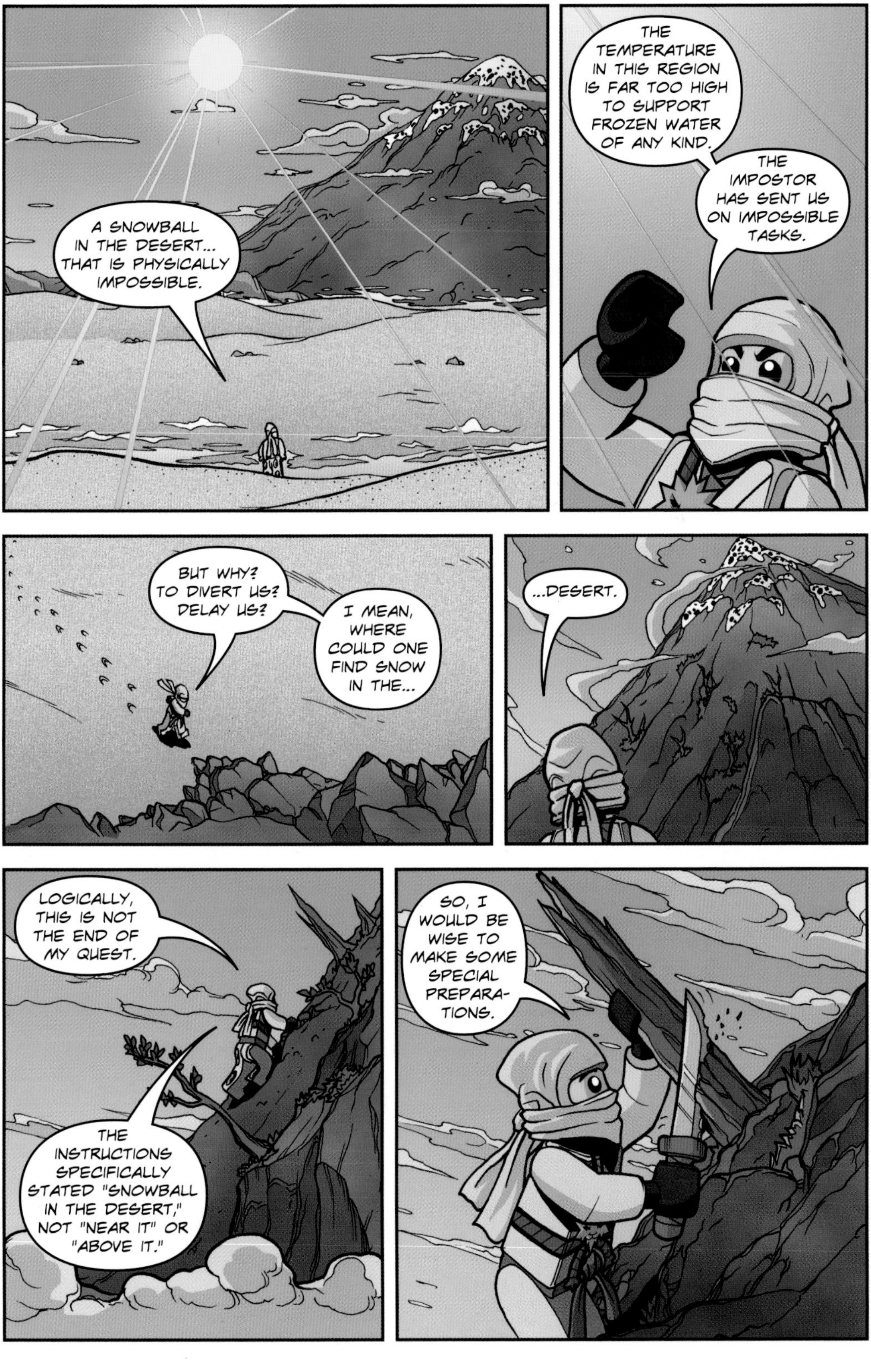
A SNOWBALL IN THE DESERT... THAT IS PHYSICALLY IMPOSSIBLE.
THE TEMPERATURE IN THIS REGION IS FAR TOO HIGH TO SUPPORT FROZEN WATER OF ANY KIND.
THE IMPOSTOR HAS SENT US ON IMPOSSIBLE TASKS.
BUT WHY? TO DIVERT US? DELAY US?
I MEAN, WHERE COULD ONE FIND SNOW IN THE...
...DESERT.
LOGICALLY, THIS IS NOT THE END OF MY QUEST.
THE INSTRUCTIONS SPECIFICALLY STATED "SNOWBALL IN THE DESERT," NOT "NEAR IT" OR "ABOVE IT."
SO, I WOULD BE WISE TO MAKE SOME SPECIAL PREPARA-TIONS.

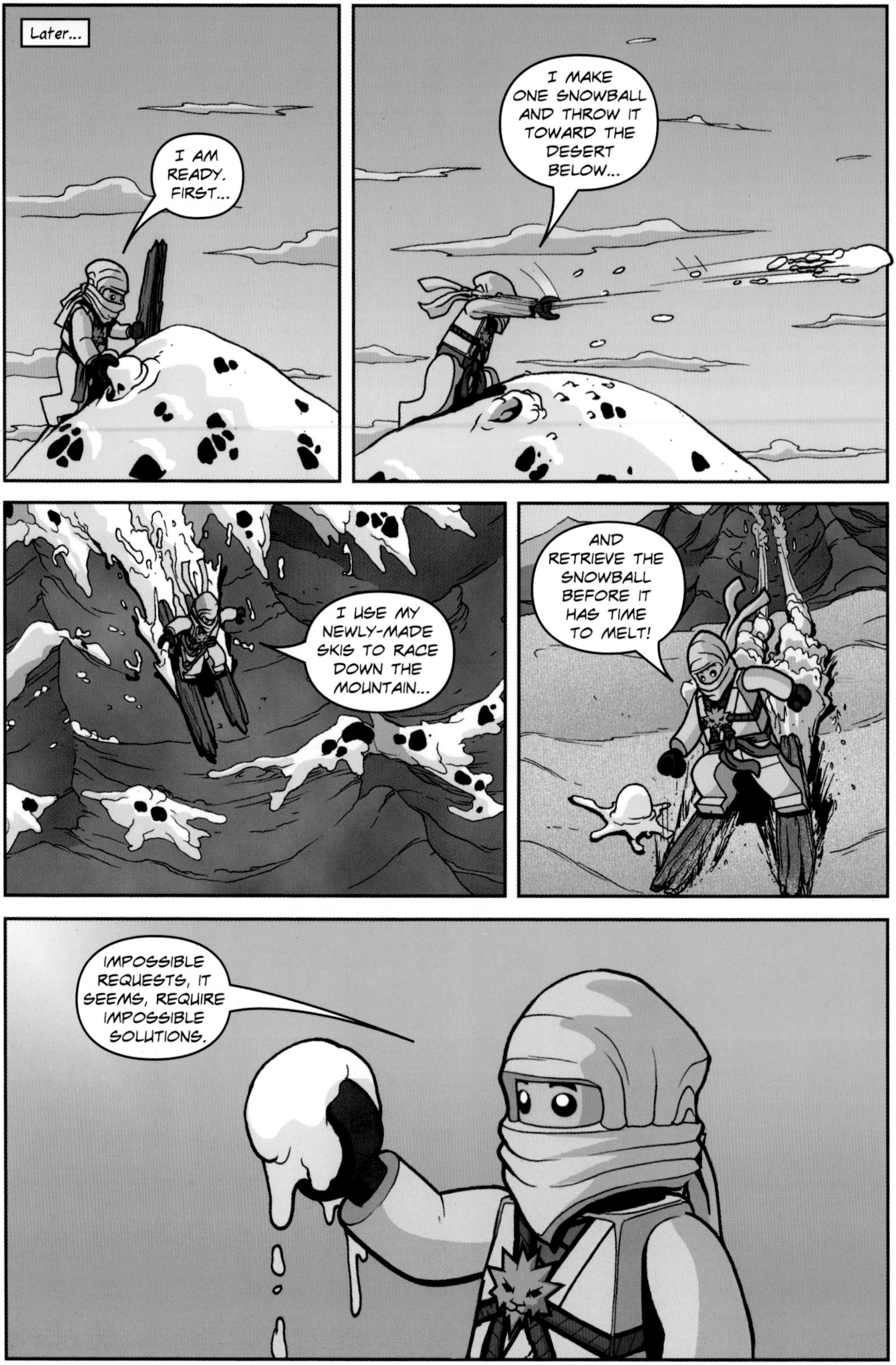
Later...
I AM READY. FIRST...
I MAKE ONE SNOWBALL AND THROW IT TOWARD THE DESERT BELOW...
I USE MY NEWLY-MADE SKIS TO RACE DOWN THE MOUNTAIN...
AND RETRIEVE THE SNOWBALL BEFORE IT HAS TIME TO MELT!
IMPOSSIBLE REQUESTS, IT SEEMS, REQUIRE IMPOSSIBLE SOLUTIONS.

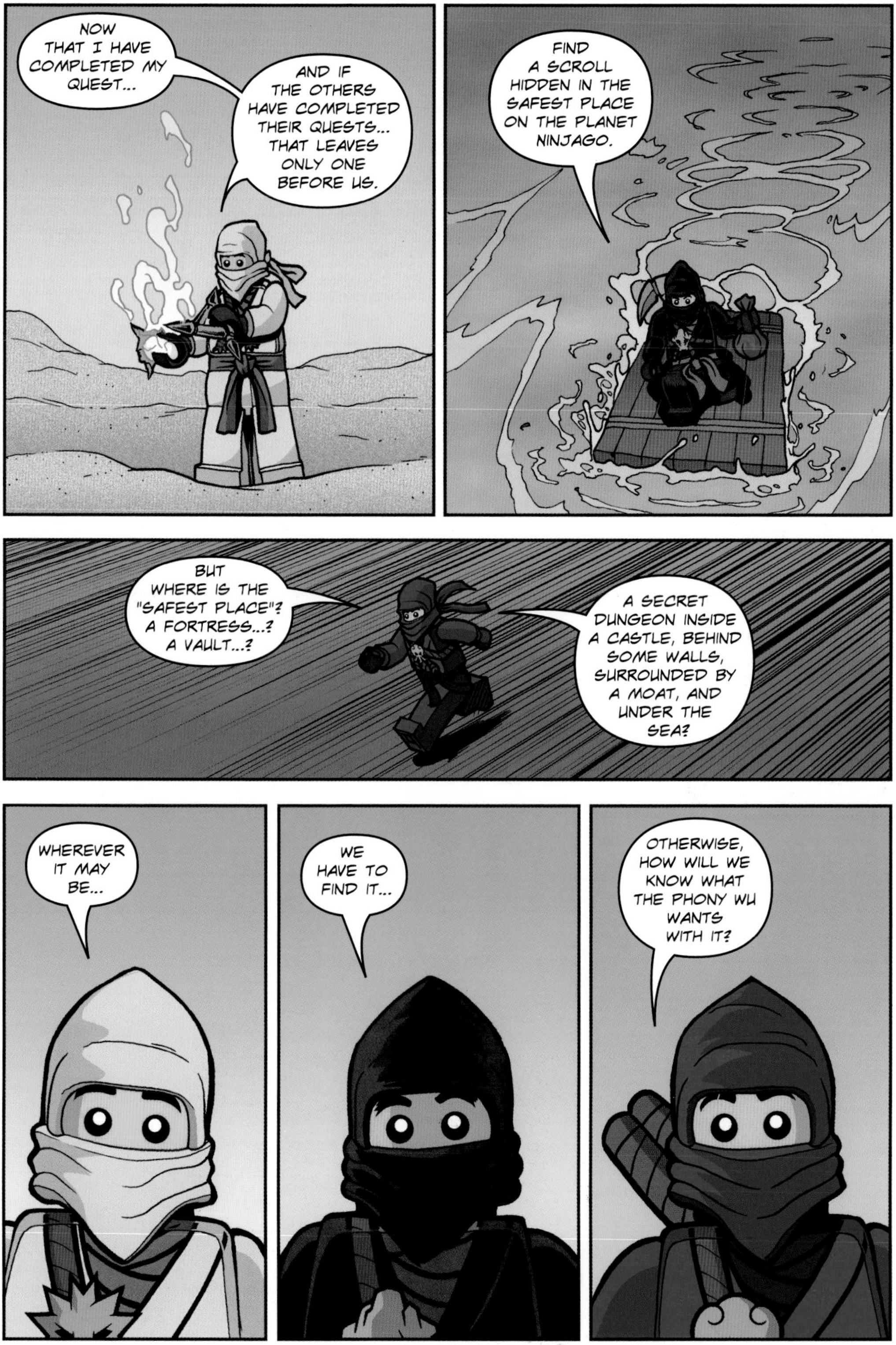
NOW THAT I HAVE COMPLETED MY QUEST...
AND IF THE OTHERS HAVE COMPLETED THEIR QUESTS... THAT LEAVES ONLY ONE BEFORE US.
FIND A SCROLL HIDDEN IN THE SAFEST PLACE ON THE PLANET NINJAGO.
BUT WHERE IS THE "SAFEST PLACE"? A FORTRESS...? A VAULT...?
A SECRET DUNGEON INSIDE A CASTLE, BEHIND SOME WALLS, SURROUNDED BY A MOAT, AND UNDER THE SEA?
WHEREVER IT MAY BE...
WE HAVE TO FIND IT...
OTHERWISE, HOW WILL WE KNOW WHAT THE PHONY WU WANTS WITH IT?

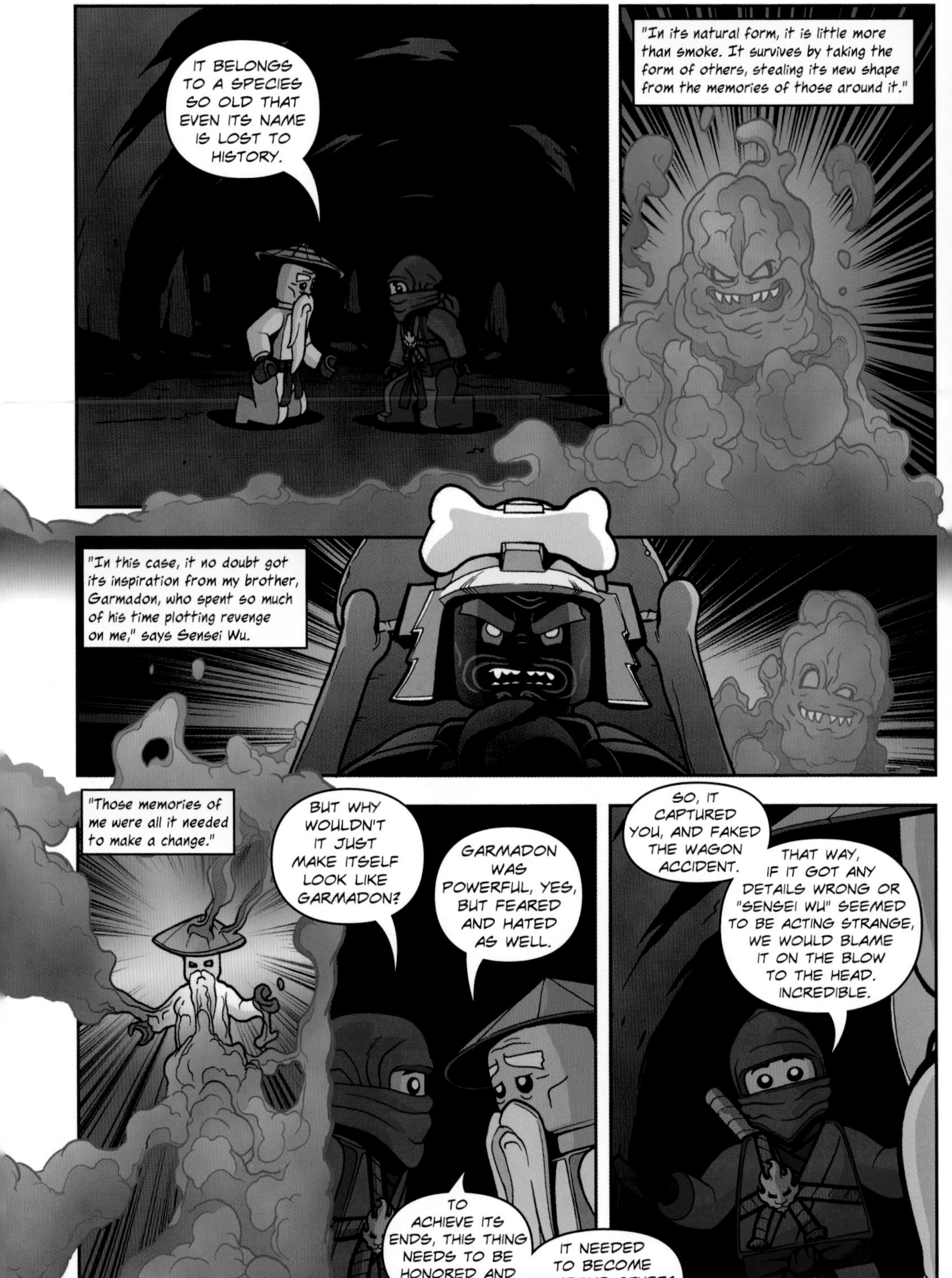
IT BELONGS TO A SPECIES SO OLD THAT EVEN ITS NAME IS LOST TO HISTORY.
"In its natural form, it is little more than smoke. It survives by taking the form of others, stealing its new shape from the memories of those around it."
"In this case, it no doubt got its inspiration from my brother, Garmadon, who spent so much of his time plotting revenge on me," says Sensei Wu.
"Those memories of me were all it needed to make a change."
BUT WHY WOULDN'T IT JUST MAKE ITSELF LOOK LIKE GARMADON?
GARMADON WAS POWERFUL, YES, BUT FEARED AND HATED AS WELL.
TO ACHIEVE ITS ENDS, THIS THING NEEDS TO BE HONORED AND ADMIRED.
IT NEEDED TO BECOME SOMEONE OTHERS WOULD TRUST.
SO, IT CAPTURED YOU, AND FAKED THE WAGON ACCIDENT.
THAT WAY, IF IT GOT ANY DETAILS WRONG OR "SENSEI WU" SEEMED TO BE ACTING STRANGE, WE WOULD BLAME IT ON THE BLOW TO THE HEAD. INCREDIBLE.

ALL RIGHT. WHAT DOES IT WANT, AND HOW DO WE STOP IT?

IT WANTS NINJAGO... DOESN'T EVERYONE, IT SEEMS? AS FOR STOPPING IT, I HAVE A FEW IDEAS...

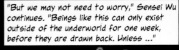

"But we may not need to worry," Sensei Wu continues. "Beings like this can only exist outside of the underworld for one week, before they are drawn back. Unless ..."

UNLESS ...?

IT WOULD NEED FOUR ITEMS: DUST FROM A RIVER, A SNOWBALL FROM THE DESERT, THE SCALE OF AN ANGRY DRAGON, AND A SCROLL TAKEN FROM THE SAFEST PLACE ON THE PLANET.

WITH THOSE, IT COULD MAKE ITS STAY HERE PERMANENT.

THAT'S A RELIEF.

I MEAN, WHO WOULD BE DUMB ENOUGH TO GO COLLECT STUFF LIKE THAT?

I SEE WE ALL GOT OUR ITEMS. THAT JUST LEAVES THE SCROLL.

AND WE STILL DON'T KNOW WHAT HE WANTS ALL THIS FOR.

MIGHT I SUGGEST, NOTHING GOOD?

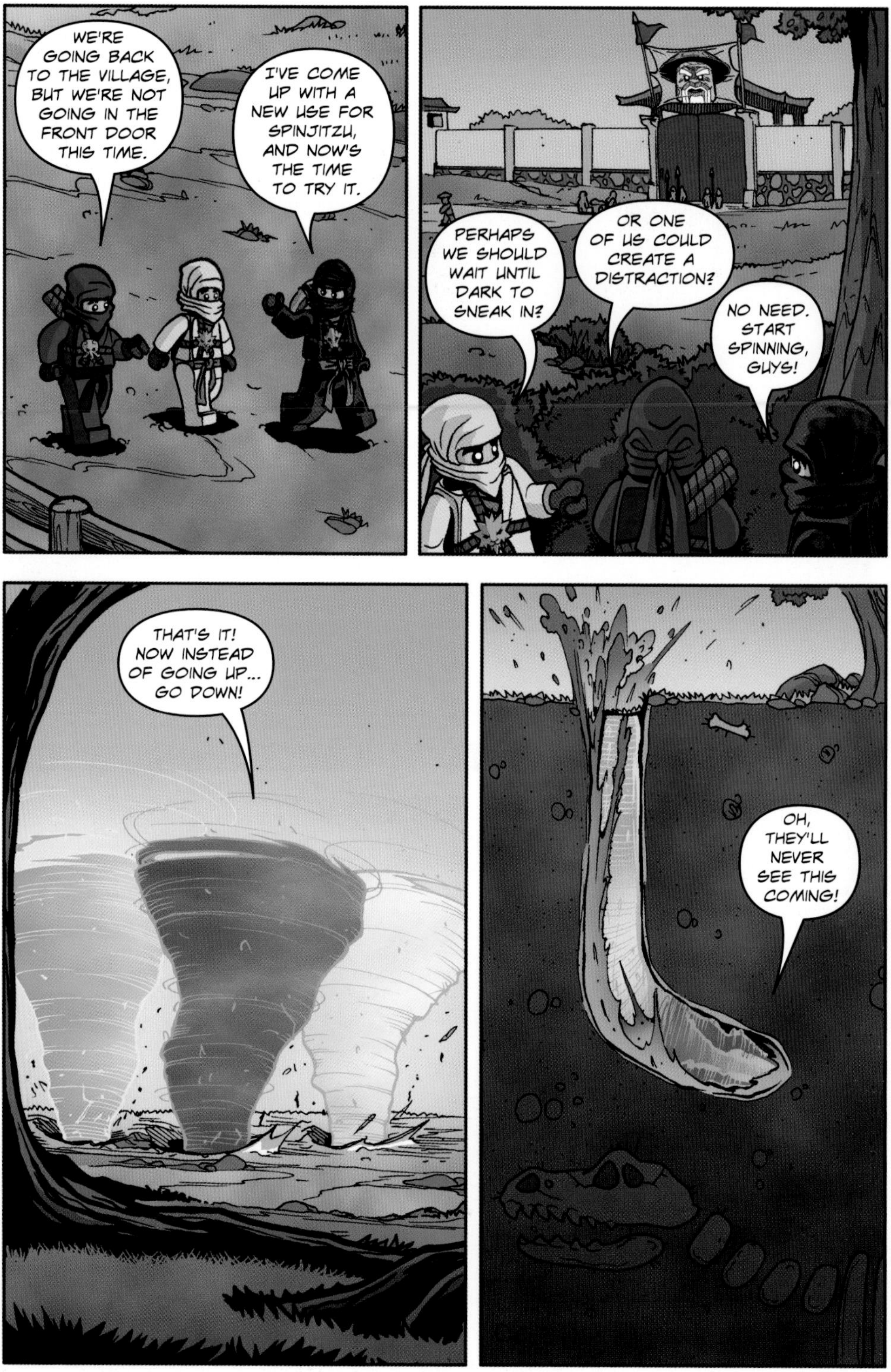
WE'RE GOING BACK TO THE VILLAGE, BUT WE'RE NOT GOING IN THE FRONT DOOR THIS TIME.
I'VE COME UP WITH A NEW USE FOR SPINJITZU, AND NOW'S THE TIME TO TRY IT.
PERHAPS WE SHOULD WAIT UNTIL DARK TO SNEAK IN?
OR ONE OF US COULD CREATE A DISTRACTION?
NO NEED. START SPINNING, GUYS!
THAT'S IT! NOW INSTEAD OF GOING UP... GO DOWN!
OH, THEY'LL NEVER SEE THIS COMING!

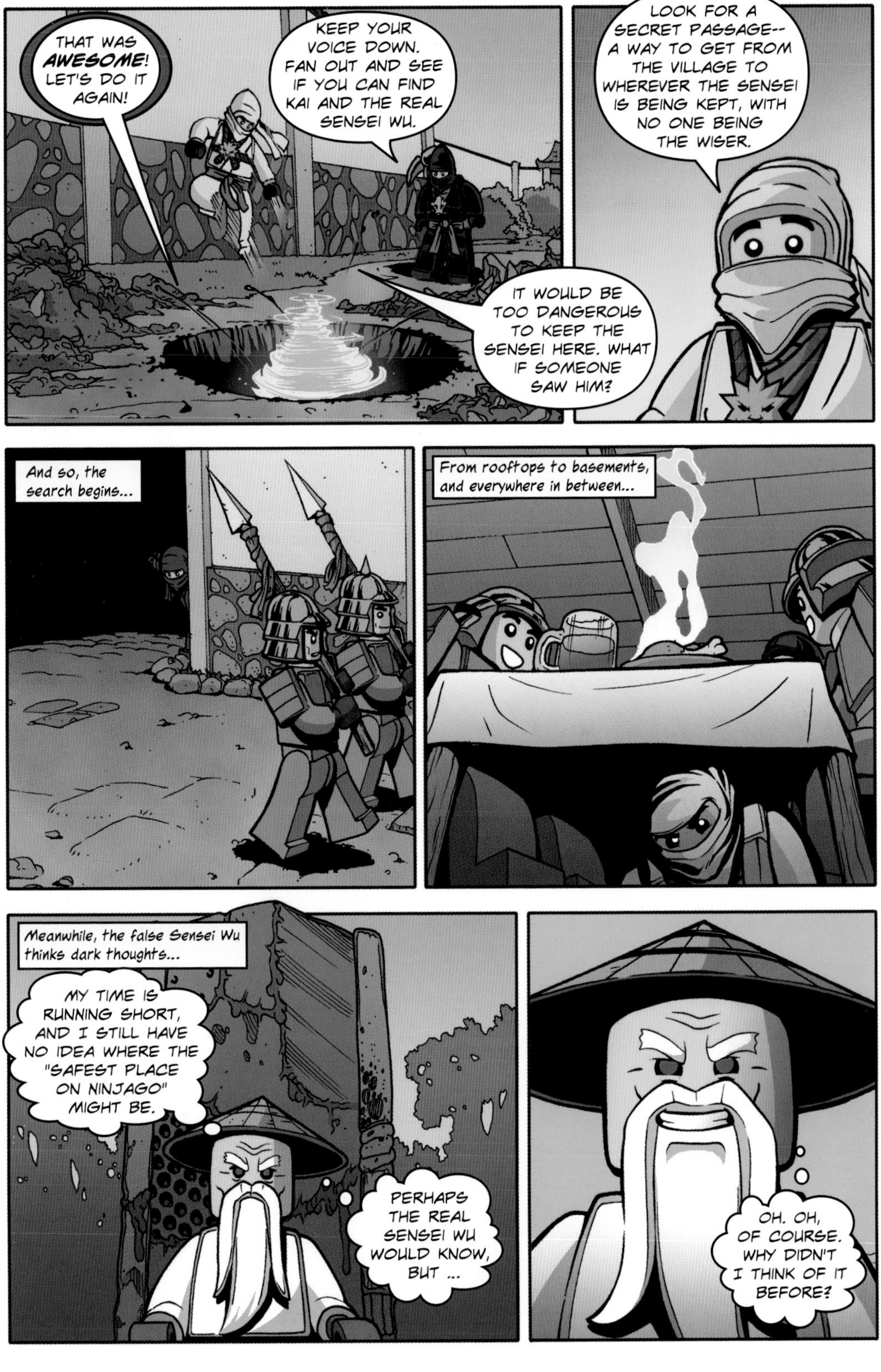
THAT WAS **AWESOME**! LET'S DO IT AGAIN!
KEEP YOUR VOICE DOWN. FAN OUT AND SEE IF YOU CAN FIND KAI AND THE REAL SENSEI WU.
IT WOULD BE TOO DANGEROUS TO KEEP THE SENSEI HERE. WHAT IF SOMEONE SAW HIM?
LOOK FOR A SECRET PASSAGE-- A WAY TO GET FROM THE VILLAGE TO WHEREVER THE SENSEI IS BEING KEPT, WITH NO ONE BEING THE WISER.
And so, the search begins...
From rooftops to basements, and everywhere in between...
Meanwhile, the false Sensei Wu thinks dark thoughts...
MY TIME IS RUNNING SHORT, AND I STILL HAVE NO IDEA WHERE THE "SAFEST PLACE ON NINJAGO" MIGHT BE.
PERHAPS THE REAL SENSEI WU WOULD KNOW, BUT ...
OH. OH, OF COURSE. WHY DIDN'T I THINK OF IT BEFORE?

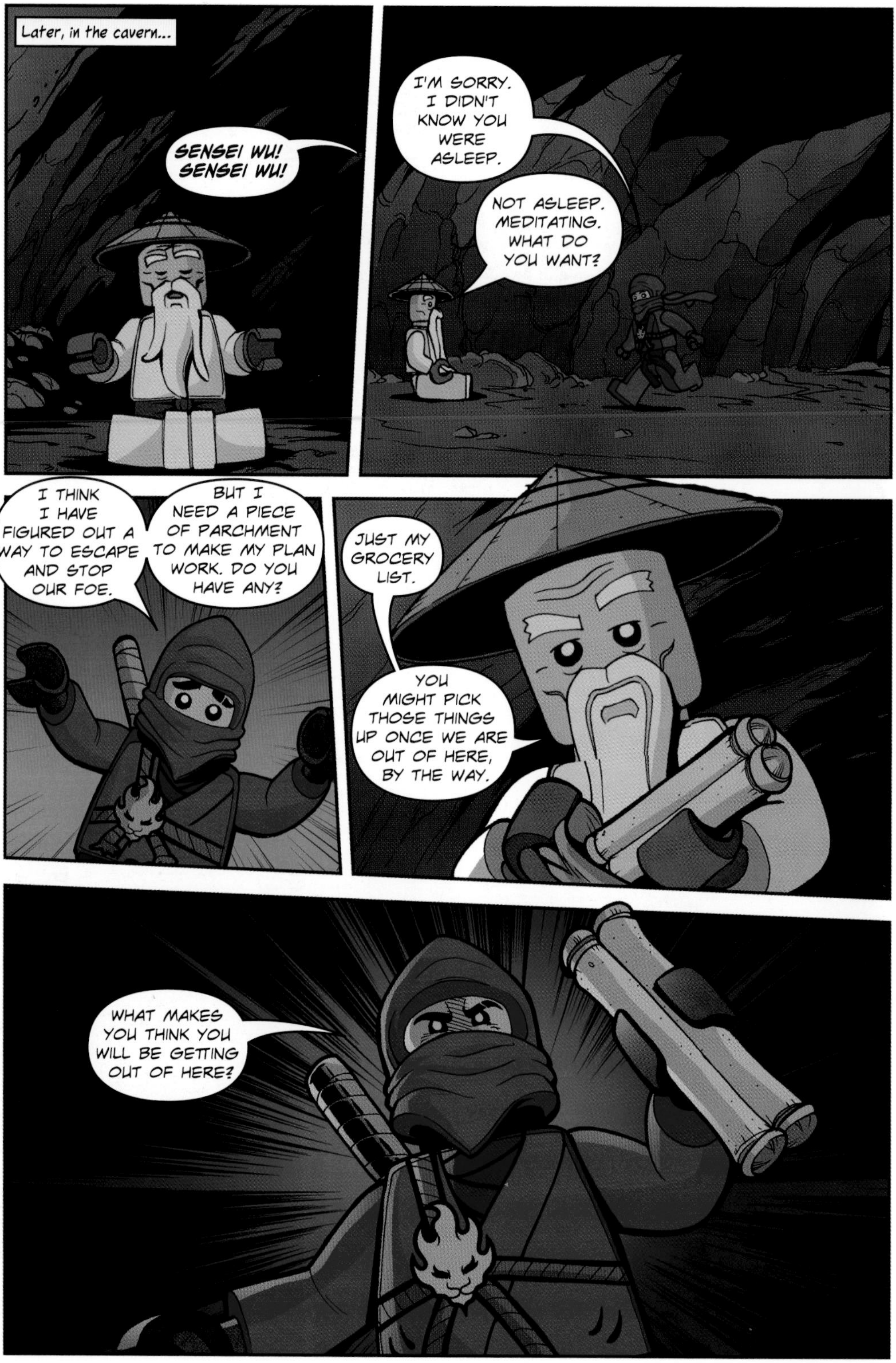
Later, in the cavern...
SENSEI WU! SENSEI WU!
I'M SORRY. I DIDN'T KNOW YOU WERE ASLEEP.
NOT ASLEEP. MEDITATING. WHAT DO YOU WANT?
I THINK I HAVE FIGURED OUT A WAY TO ESCAPE AND STOP OUR FOE.
BUT I NEED A PIECE OF PARCHMENT TO MAKE MY PLAN WORK. DO YOU HAVE ANY?
JUST MY GROCERY LIST.
YOU MIGHT PICK THOSE THINGS UP ONCE WE ARE OUT OF HERE, BY THE WAY.
WHAT MAKES YOU THINK YOU WILL BE GETTING OUT OF HERE?

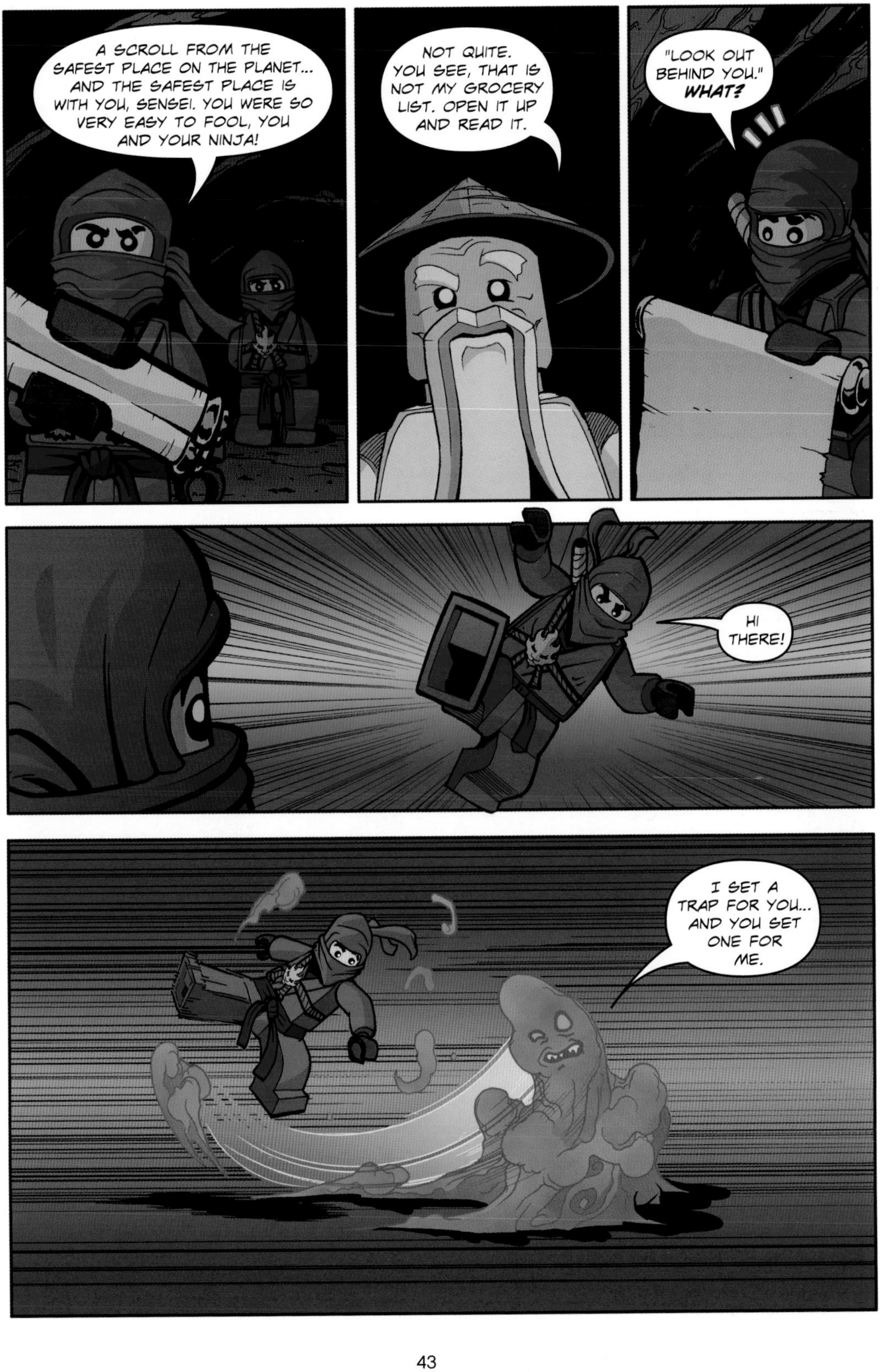
A SCROLL FROM THE SAFEST PLACE ON THE PLANET... AND THE SAFEST PLACE IS WITH YOU, SENSEI. YOU WERE SO VERY EASY TO FOOL, YOU AND YOUR NINJA!
NOT QUITE. YOU SEE, THAT IS NOT MY GROCERY LIST. OPEN IT UP AND READ IT.
"LOOK OUT BEHIND YOU." ***WHAT?***
HI THERE!
I SET A TRAP FOR YOU... AND YOU SET ONE FOR ME.

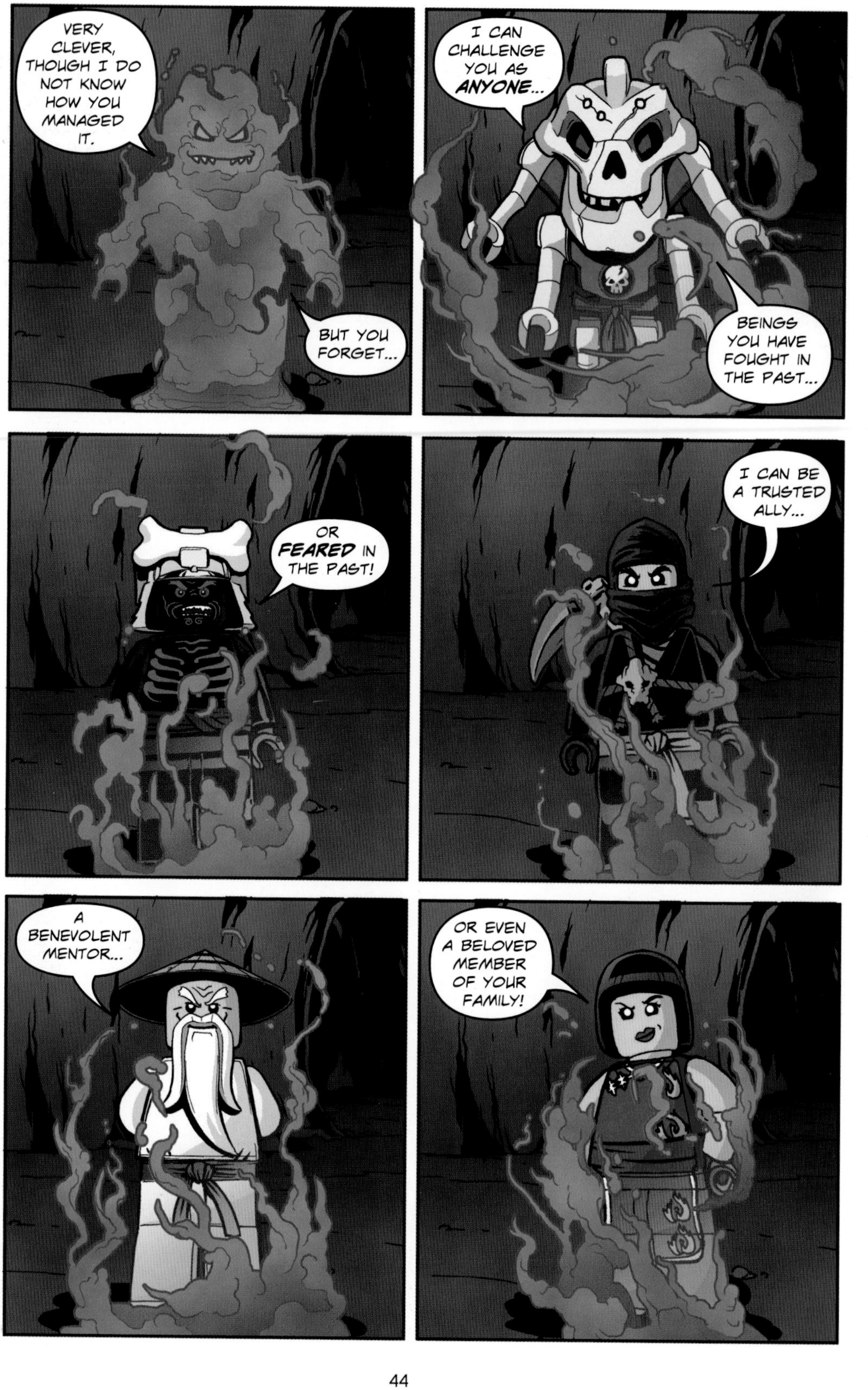
VERY CLEVER, THOUGH I DO NOT KNOW HOW YOU MANAGED IT.
BUT YOU FORGET...
I CAN CHALLENGE YOU AS ANYONE...
BEINGS YOU HAVE FOUGHT IN THE PAST...
OR FEARED IN THE PAST!
I CAN BE A TRUSTED ALLY...
A BENEVOLENT MENTOR...
OR EVEN A BELOVED MEMBER OF YOUR FAMILY!

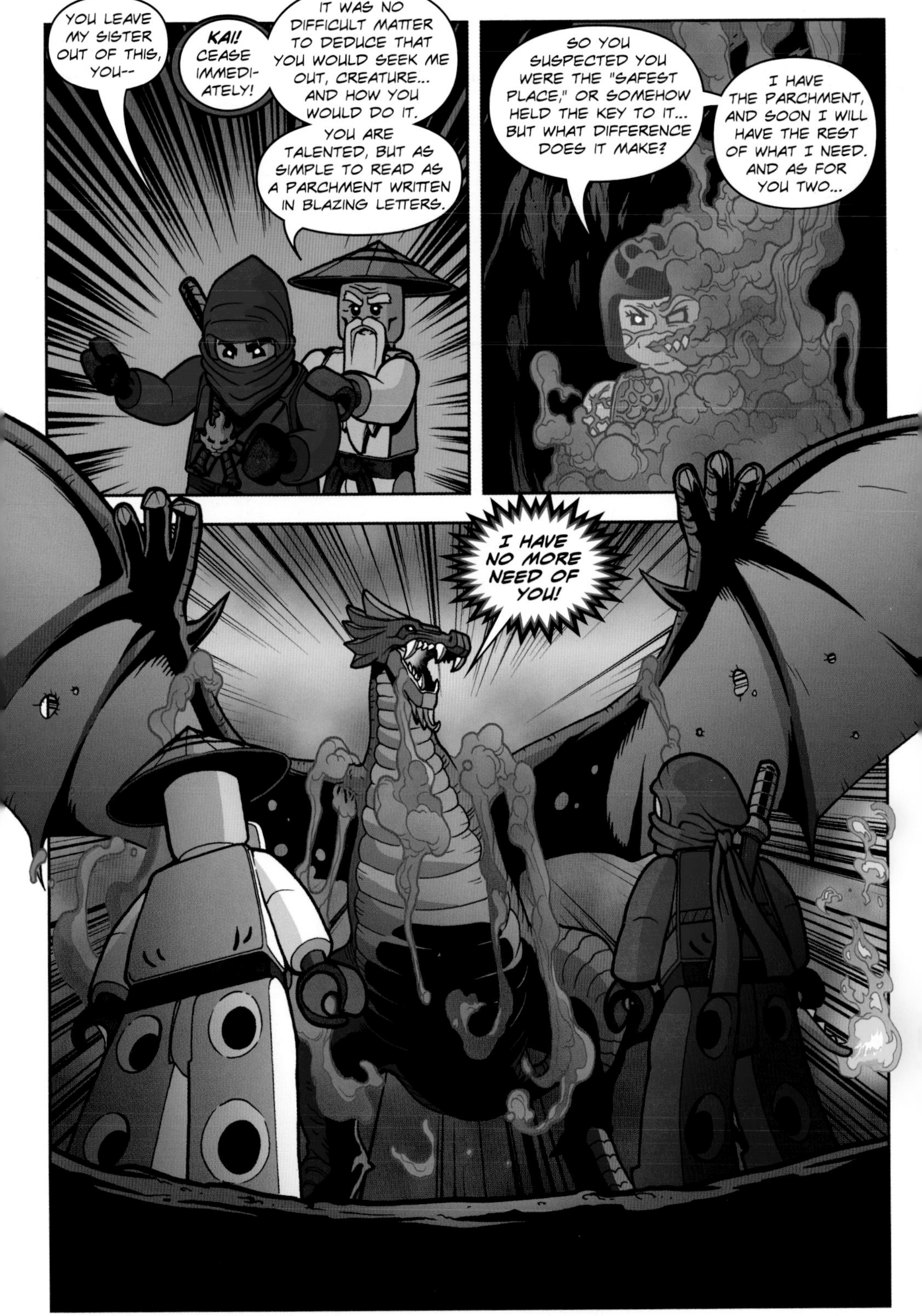
YOU LEAVE MY SISTER OUT OF THIS, YOU--
KAI! CEASE IMMEDI-ATELY!
IT WAS NO DIFFICULT MATTER TO DEDUCE THAT YOU WOULD SEEK ME OUT, CREATURE... AND HOW YOU WOULD DO IT.
YOU ARE TALENTED, BUT AS SIMPLE TO READ AS A PARCHMENT WRITTEN IN BLAZING LETTERS.
SO YOU SUSPECTED YOU WERE THE "SAFEST PLACE," OR SOMEHOW HELD THE KEY TO IT... BUT WHAT DIFFERENCE DOES IT MAKE?
I HAVE THE PARCHMENT, AND SOON I WILL HAVE THE REST OF WHAT I NEED. AND AS FOR YOU TWO...
I HAVE NO MORE NEED OF YOU!

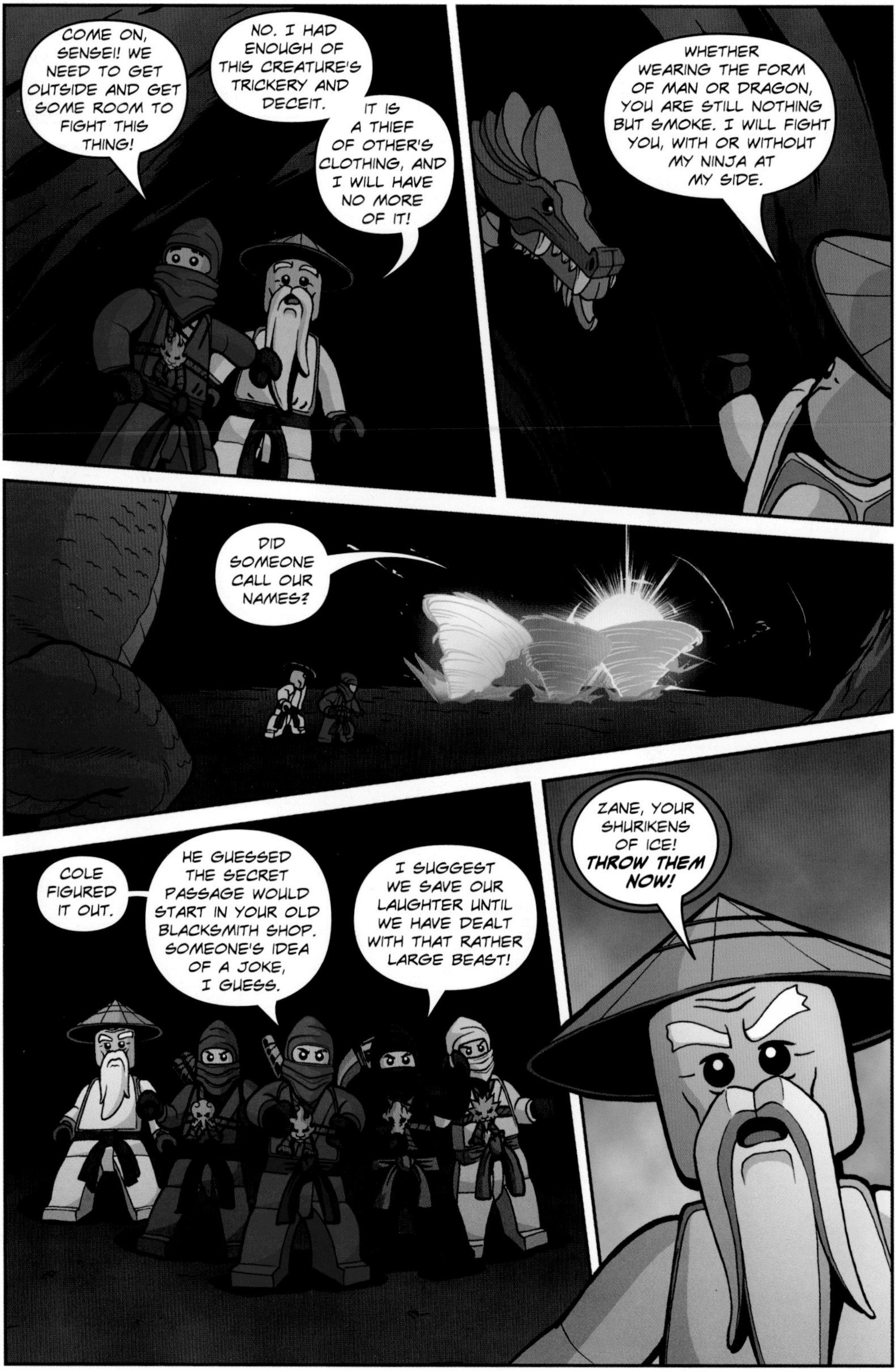
COME ON, SENSEI! WE NEED TO GET OUTSIDE AND GET SOME ROOM TO FIGHT THIS THING!
NO. I HAD ENOUGH OF THIS CREATURE'S TRICKERY AND DECEIT.
IT IS A THIEF OF OTHER'S CLOTHING, AND I WILL HAVE NO MORE OF IT!
WHETHER WEARING THE FORM OF MAN OR DRAGON, YOU ARE STILL NOTHING BUT SMOKE. I WILL FIGHT YOU, WITH OR WITHOUT MY NINJA AT MY SIDE.
DID SOMEONE CALL OUR NAMES?
COLE FIGURED IT OUT.
HE GUESSED THE SECRET PASSAGE WOULD START IN YOUR OLD BLACKSMITH SHOP. SOMEONE'S IDEA OF A JOKE, I GUESS.
I SUGGEST WE SAVE OUR LAUGHTER UNTIL WE HAVE DEALT WITH THAT RATHER LARGE BEAST!
ZANE, YOUR SHURIKENS OF ICE! **THROW THEM NOW!**

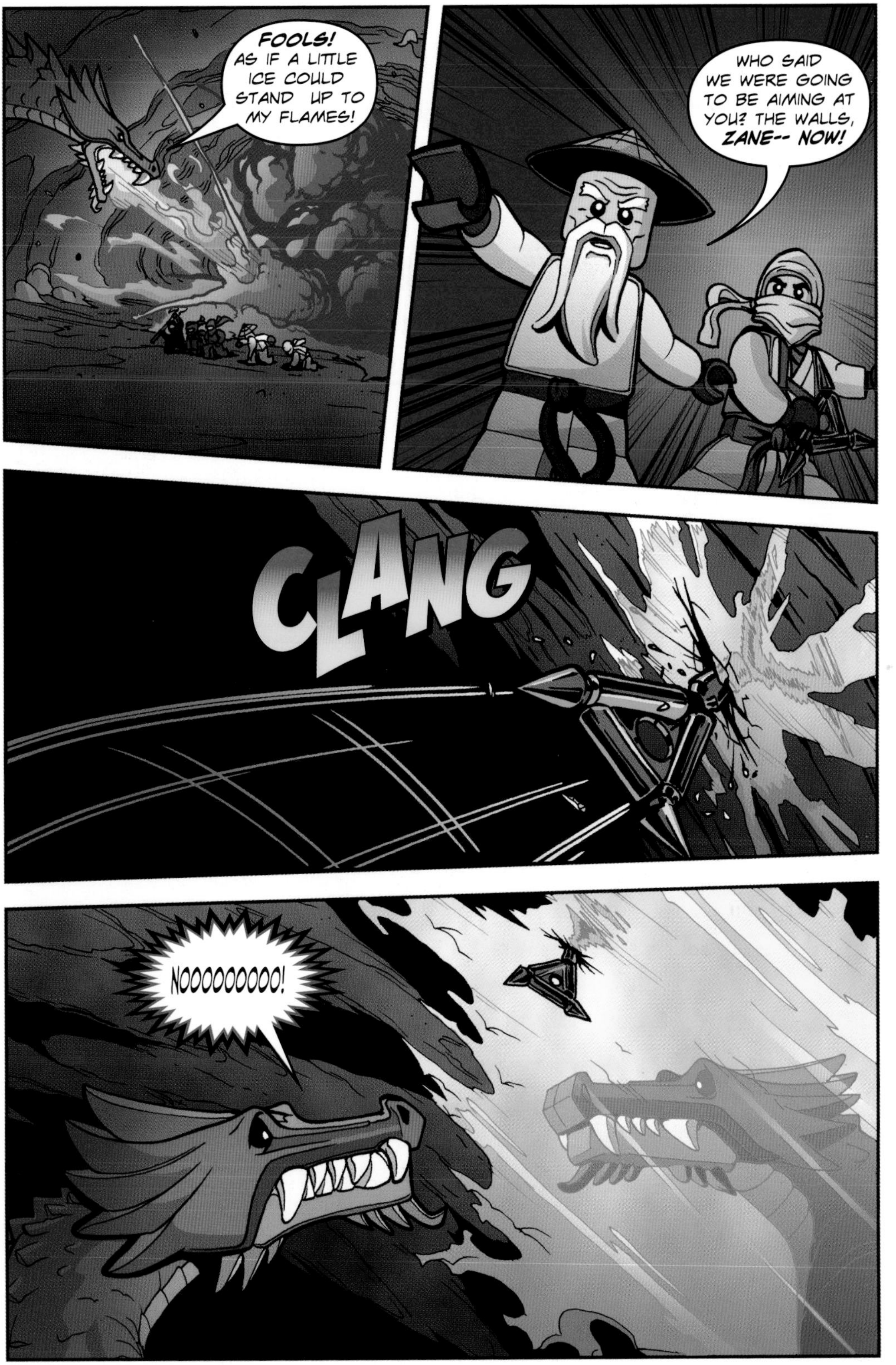
FOOLS! AS IF A LITTLE ICE COULD STAND UP TO MY FLAMES!
WHO SAID WE WERE GOING TO BE AIMING AT YOU? THE WALLS, ZANE-- NOW!
CLANG
NOOOOOOOOO!

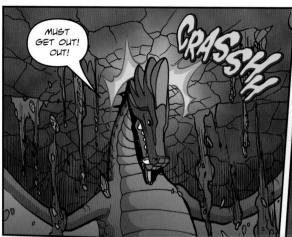

MUST GET OUT! OUT!

CRASSHH

WHAT JUST HAPPENED?

I THOUGHT I RECALLED THE WEAKNESS OF ITS SPECIES-- IT CANNOT STAND TO SEE ITS OWN REFLECTION.

WHICH IT DID, IN MY ICE--

SO IS IT OVER? HAVE WE WON?

KA-BLAMM

YAAARRGGH!

I THINK NOT.

HOW DO WE FIGHT SOMETHING THAT CAN BE ANYTHING IT WANTS TO BE?

BY REMEMBERING ALWAYS WHAT WE ARE, AND WHAT WE CAN DO.

WHAT WE CAN DO...? ZANE, I THINK I MIGHT HAVE AN IDEA!

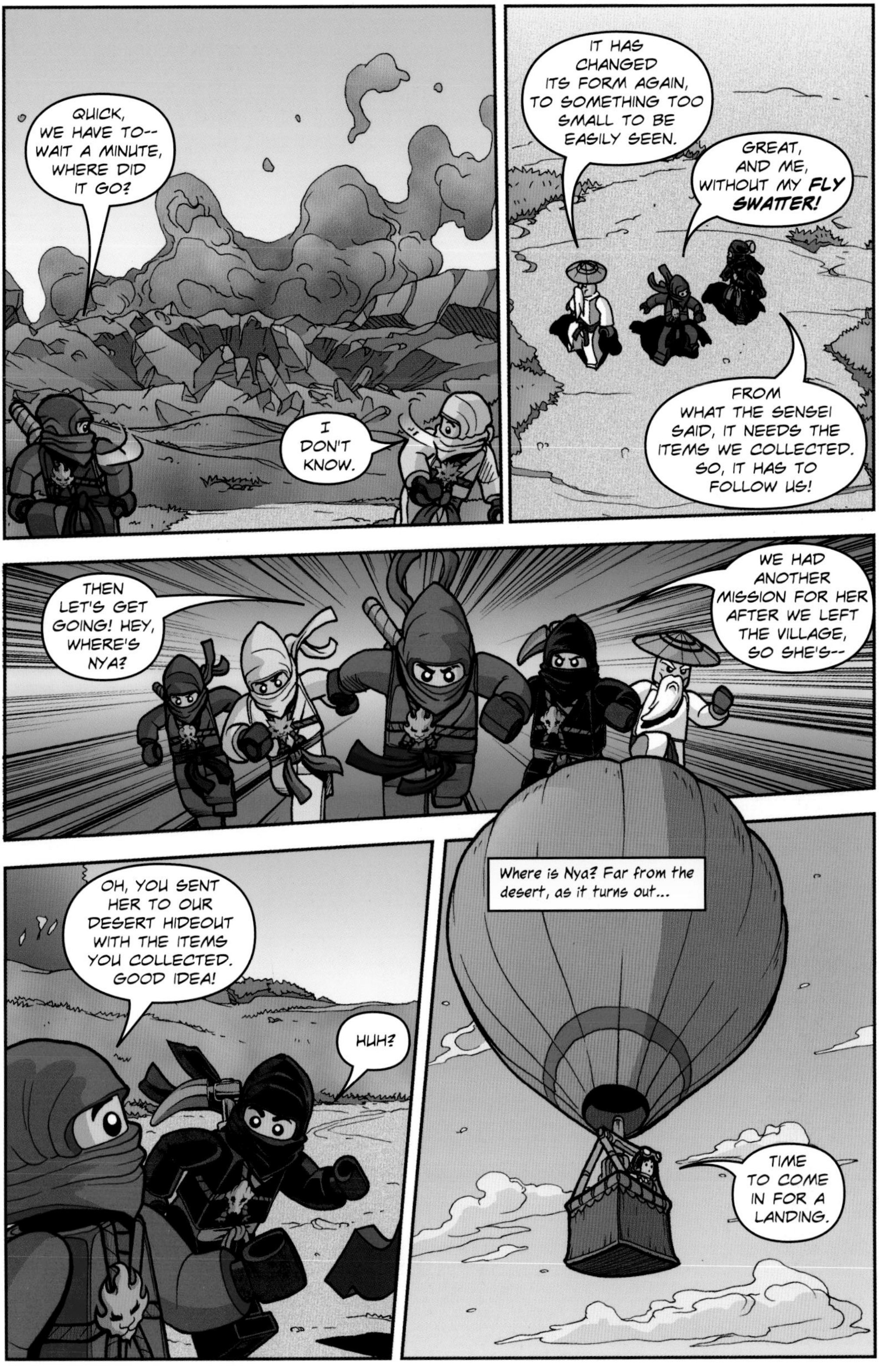
QUICK, WE HAVE TO-- WAIT A MINUTE, WHERE DID IT GO?
I DON'T KNOW.
IT HAS CHANGED ITS FORM AGAIN, TO SOMETHING TOO SMALL TO BE EASILY SEEN.
GREAT, AND ME, WITHOUT MY FLY SWATTER!
FROM WHAT THE SENSEI SAID, IT NEEDS THE ITEMS WE COLLECTED. SO, IT HAS TO FOLLOW US!
THEN LET'S GET GOING! HEY, WHERE'S NYA?
WE HAD ANOTHER MISSION FOR HER AFTER WE LEFT THE VILLAGE, SO SHE'S--
OH, YOU SENT HER TO OUR DESERT HIDEOUT WITH THE ITEMS YOU COLLECTED. GOOD IDEA!
HUH?
Where is Nya? Far from the desert, as it turns out...
TIME TO COME IN FOR A LANDING.

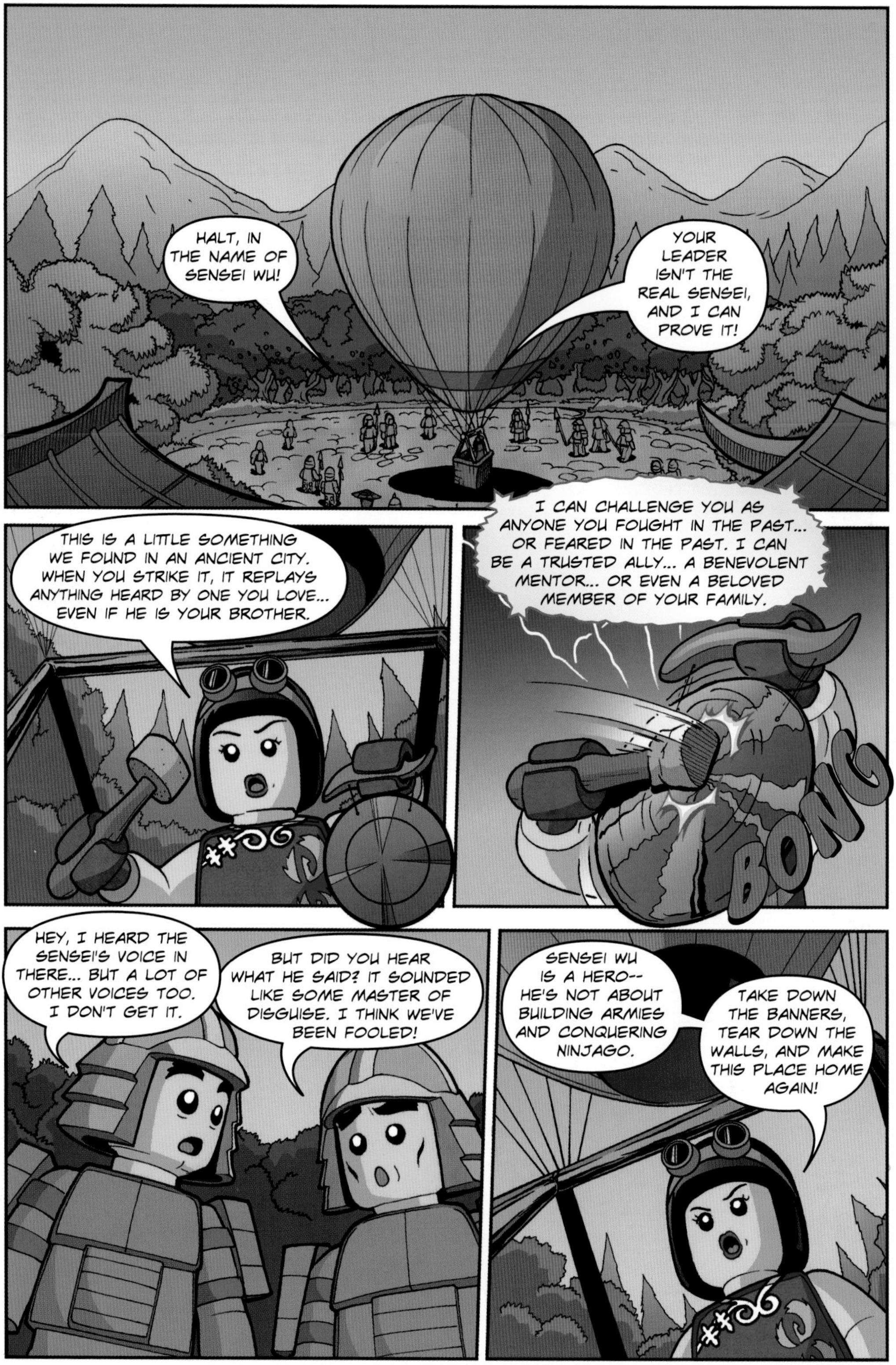
HALT, IN THE NAME OF SENSEI WU!
YOUR LEADER ISN'T THE REAL SENSEI, AND I CAN PROVE IT!
THIS IS A LITTLE SOMETHING WE FOUND IN AN ANCIENT CITY. WHEN YOU STRIKE IT, IT REPLAYS ANYTHING HEARD BY ONE YOU LOVE... EVEN IF HE IS YOUR BROTHER.
I CAN CHALLENGE YOU AS ANYONE YOU FOUGHT IN THE PAST... OR FEARED IN THE PAST. I CAN BE A TRUSTED ALLY... A BENEVOLENT MENTOR... OR EVEN A BELOVED MEMBER OF YOUR FAMILY.
BONG
HEY, I HEARD THE SENSEI'S VOICE IN THERE... BUT A LOT OF OTHER VOICES TOO. I DON'T GET IT.
BUT DID YOU HEAR WHAT HE SAID? IT SOUNDED LIKE SOME MASTER OF DISGUISE. I THINK WE'VE BEEN FOOLED!
SENSEI WU IS A HERO-- HE'S NOT ABOUT BUILDING ARMIES AND CONQUERING NINJAGO.
TAKE DOWN THE BANNERS, TEAR DOWN THE WALLS, AND MAKE THIS PLACE HOME AGAIN!

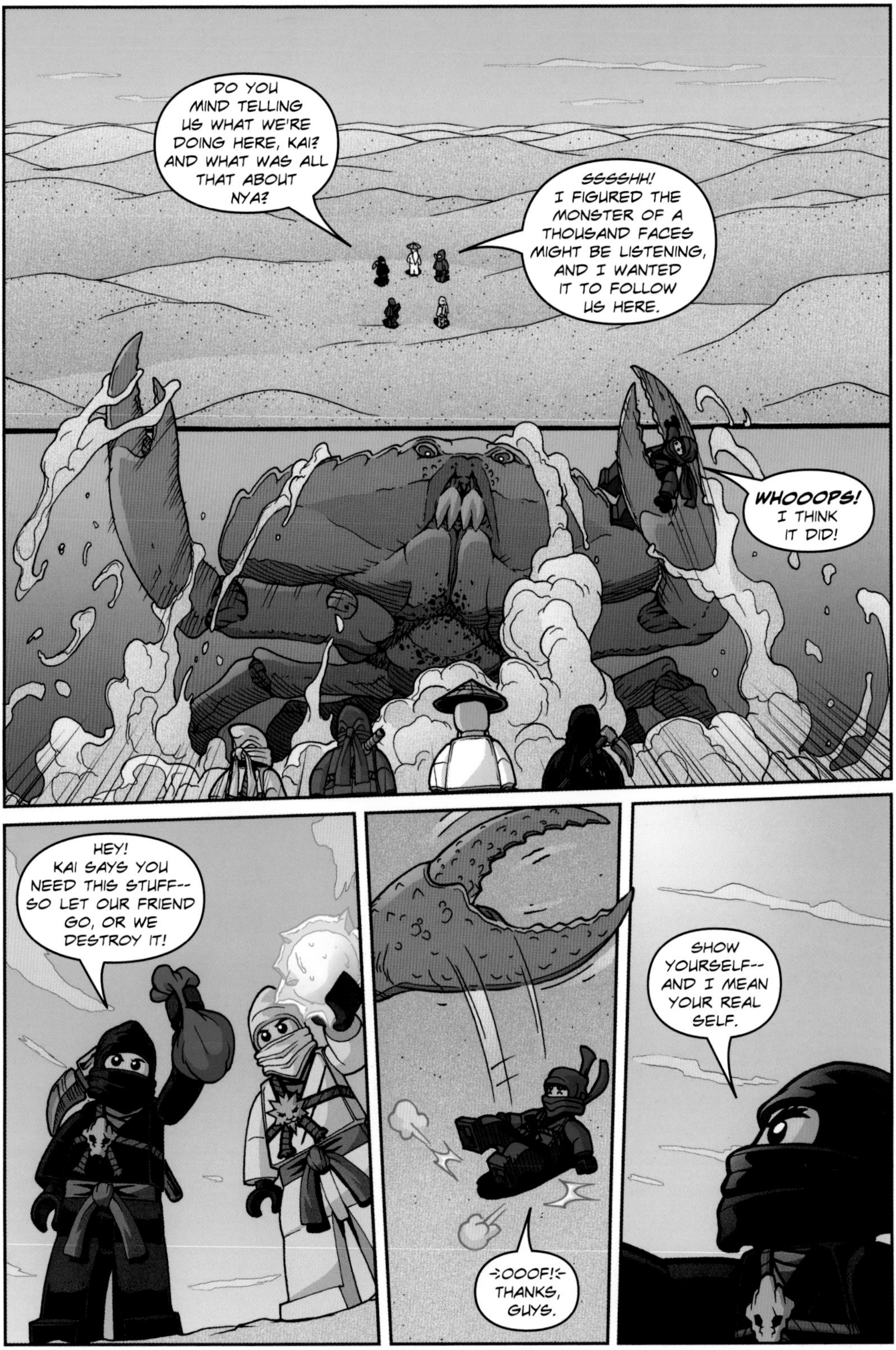
DO YOU MIND TELLING US WHAT WE'RE DOING HERE, KAI? AND WHAT WAS ALL THAT ABOUT NYA?
SSSSHH! I FIGURED THE MONSTER OF A THOUSAND FACES MIGHT BE LISTENING, AND I WANTED IT TO FOLLOW US HERE.
WHOOOPS! I THINK IT DID!
HEY! KAI SAYS YOU NEED THIS STUFF-- SO LET OUR FRIEND GO, OR WE DESTROY IT!
OOOF! THANKS, GUYS.
SHOW YOURSELF-- AND I MEAN YOUR REAL SELF.

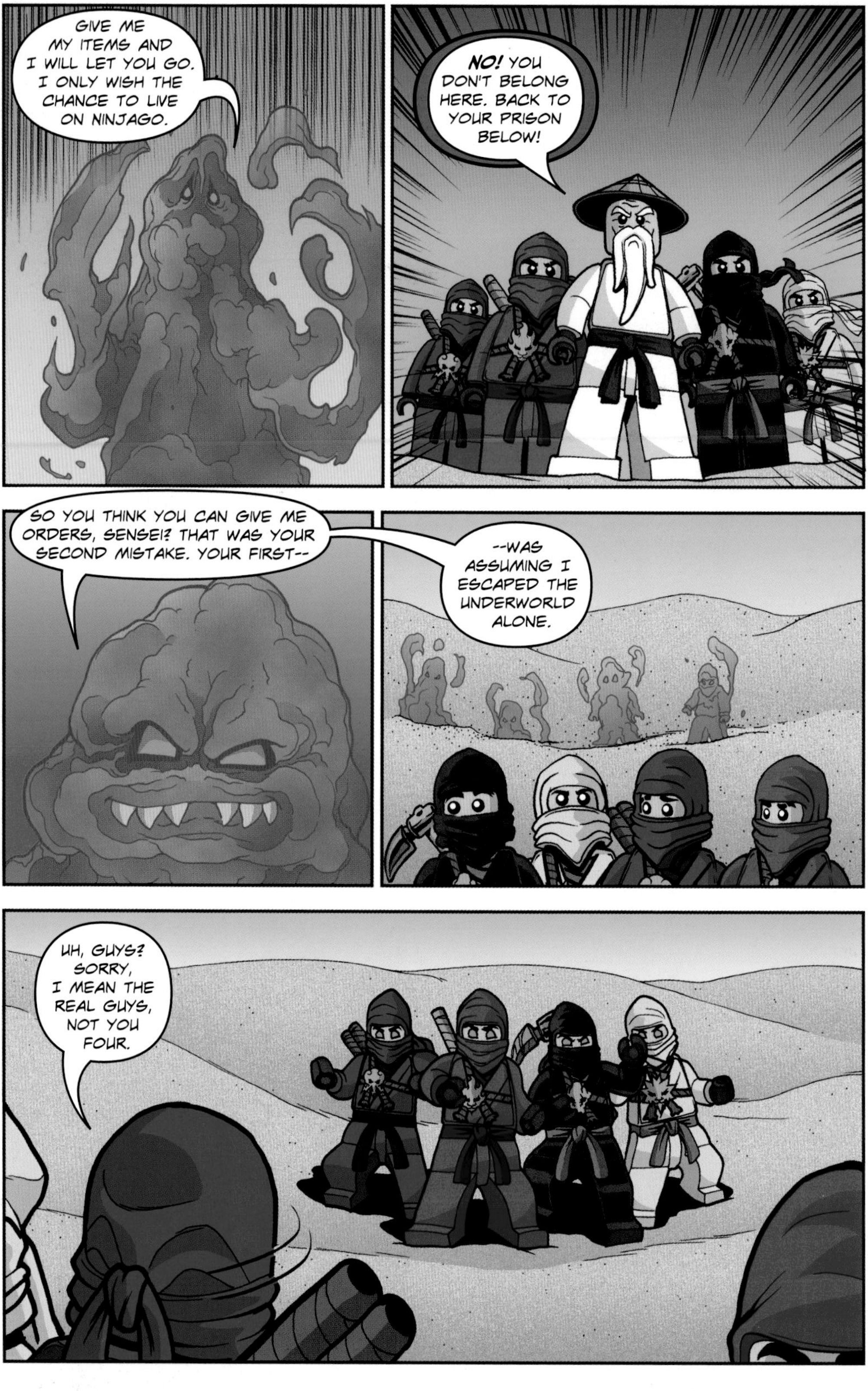
GIVE ME MY ITEMS AND I WILL LET YOU GO. I ONLY WISH THE CHANCE TO LIVE ON NINJAGO.
NO! YOU DON'T BELONG HERE. BACK TO YOUR PRISON BELOW!
SO YOU THINK YOU CAN GIVE ME ORDERS, SENSEI? THAT WAS YOUR SECOND MISTAKE. YOUR FIRST--
--WAS ASSUMING I ESCAPED THE UNDERWORLD ALONE.
UH, GUYS? SORRY, I MEAN THE REAL GUYS, NOT YOU FOUR.

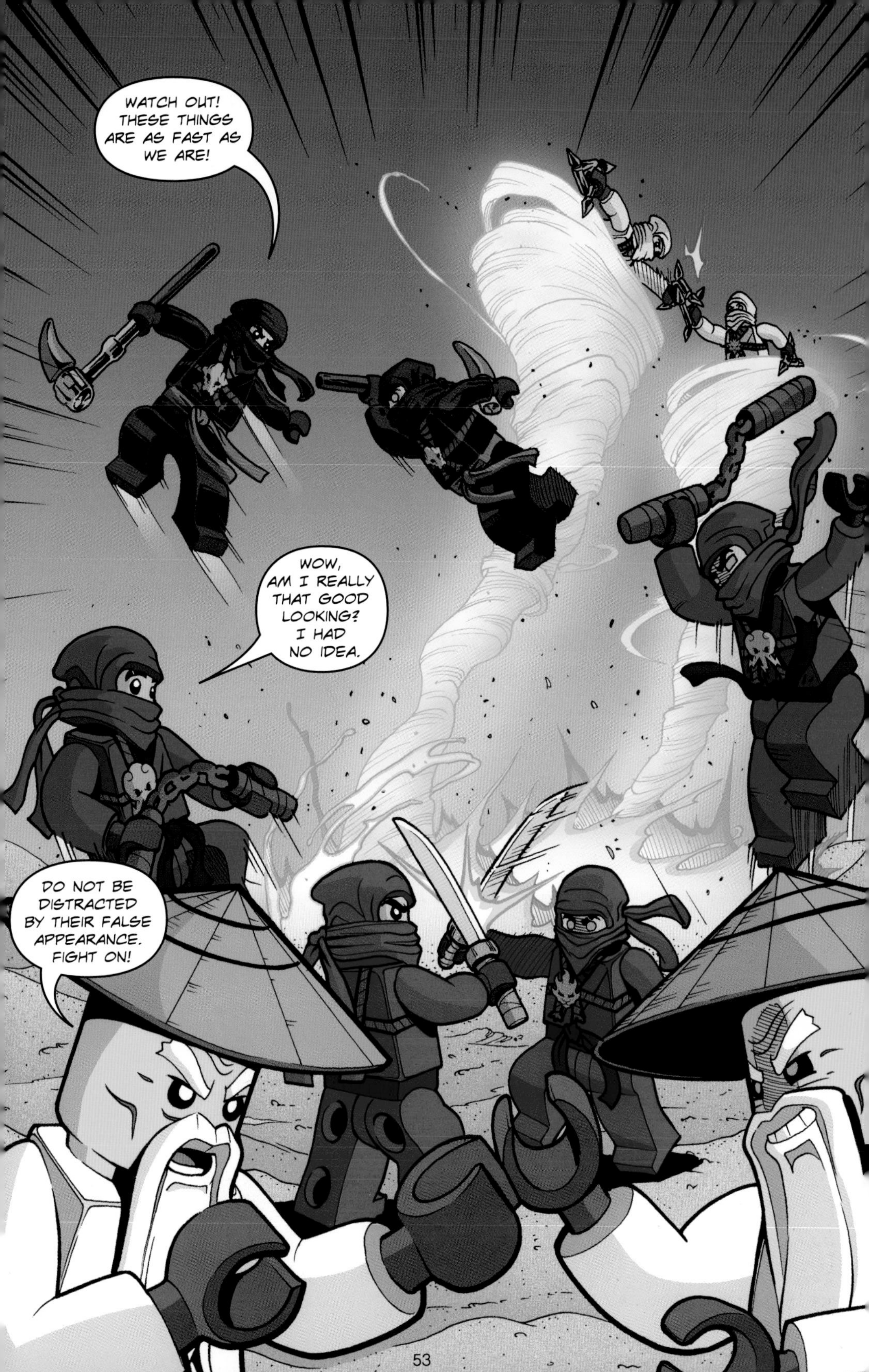
WATCH OUT! THESE THINGS ARE AS FAST AS WE ARE!
WOW, AM I REALLY THAT GOOD LOOKING? I HAD NO IDEA.
DO NOT BE DISTRACTED BY THEIR FALSE APPEARANCE. FIGHT ON!

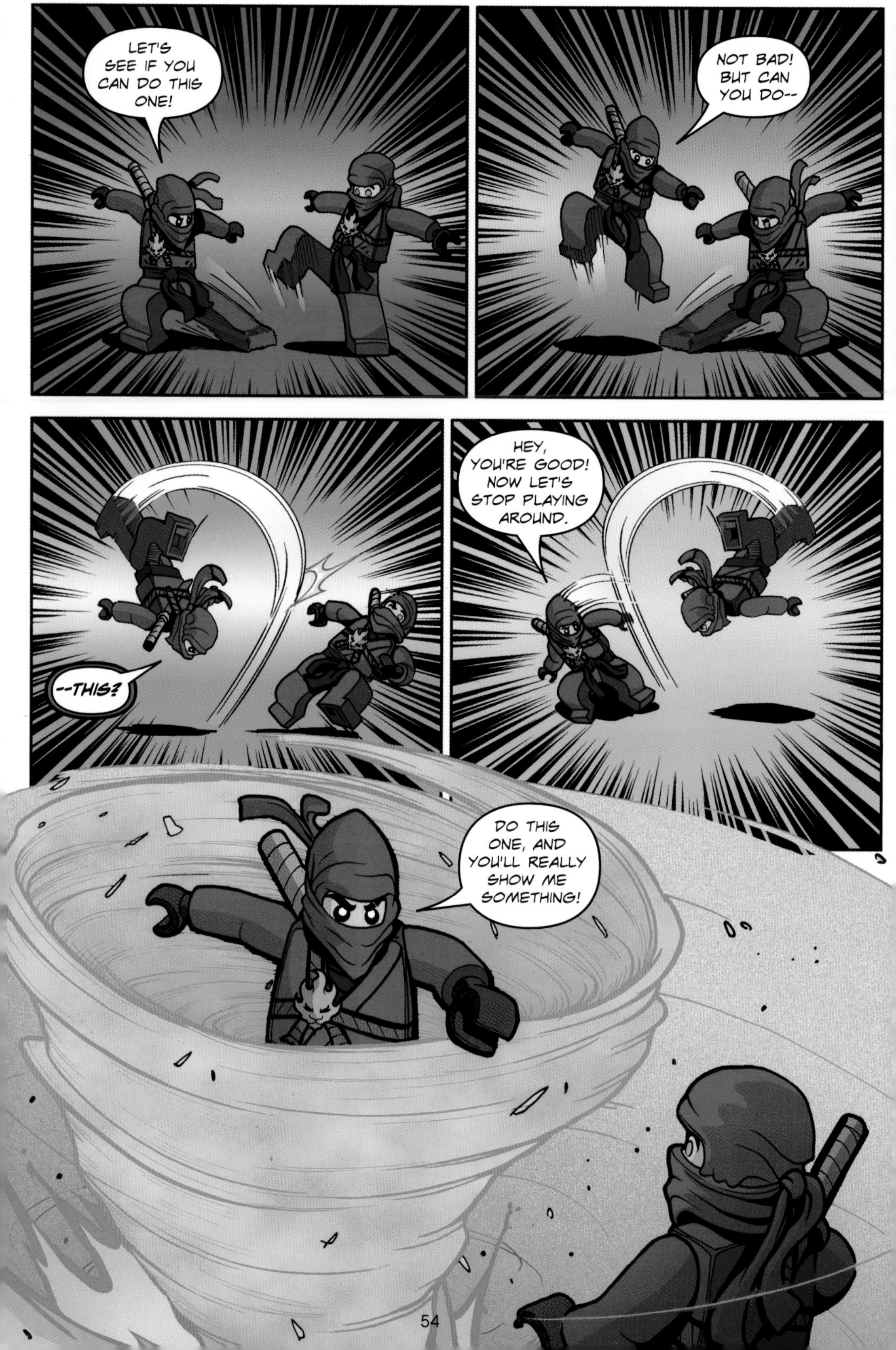

LET'S SEE IF YOU CAN DO THIS ONE!
NOT BAD! BUT CAN YOU DO--
--THIS?
HEY, YOU'RE GOOD! NOW LET'S STOP PLAYING AROUND.
DO THIS ONE, AND YOU'LL REALLY SHOW ME SOMETHING!

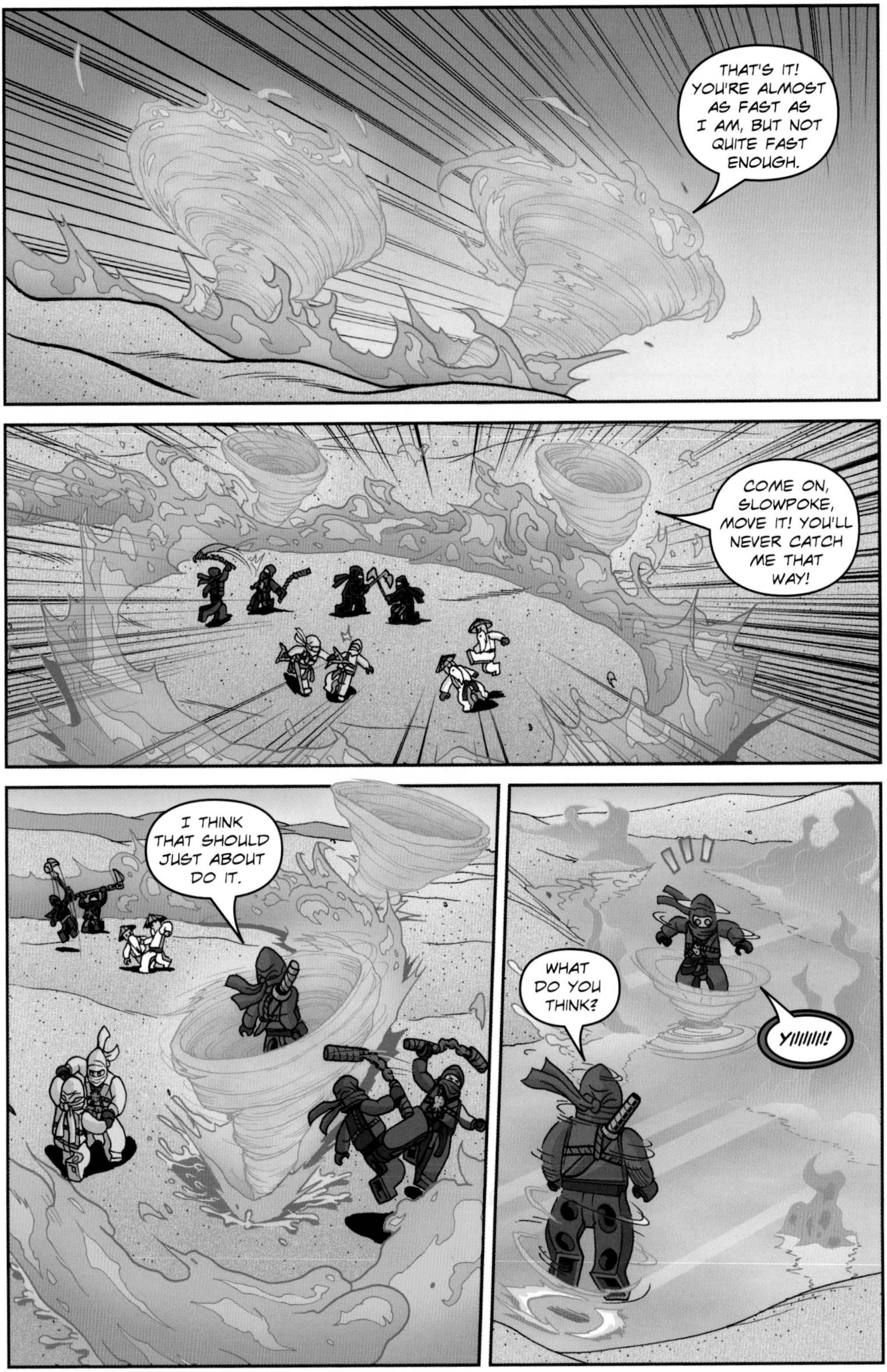
THAT'S IT! YOU'RE ALMOST AS FAST AS I AM, BUT NOT QUITE FAST ENOUGH.
COME ON, SLOWPOKE, MOVE IT! YOU'LL NEVER CATCH ME THAT WAY!
I THINK THAT SHOULD JUST ABOUT DO IT.
WHAT DO YOU THINK?
YIIIIIII!

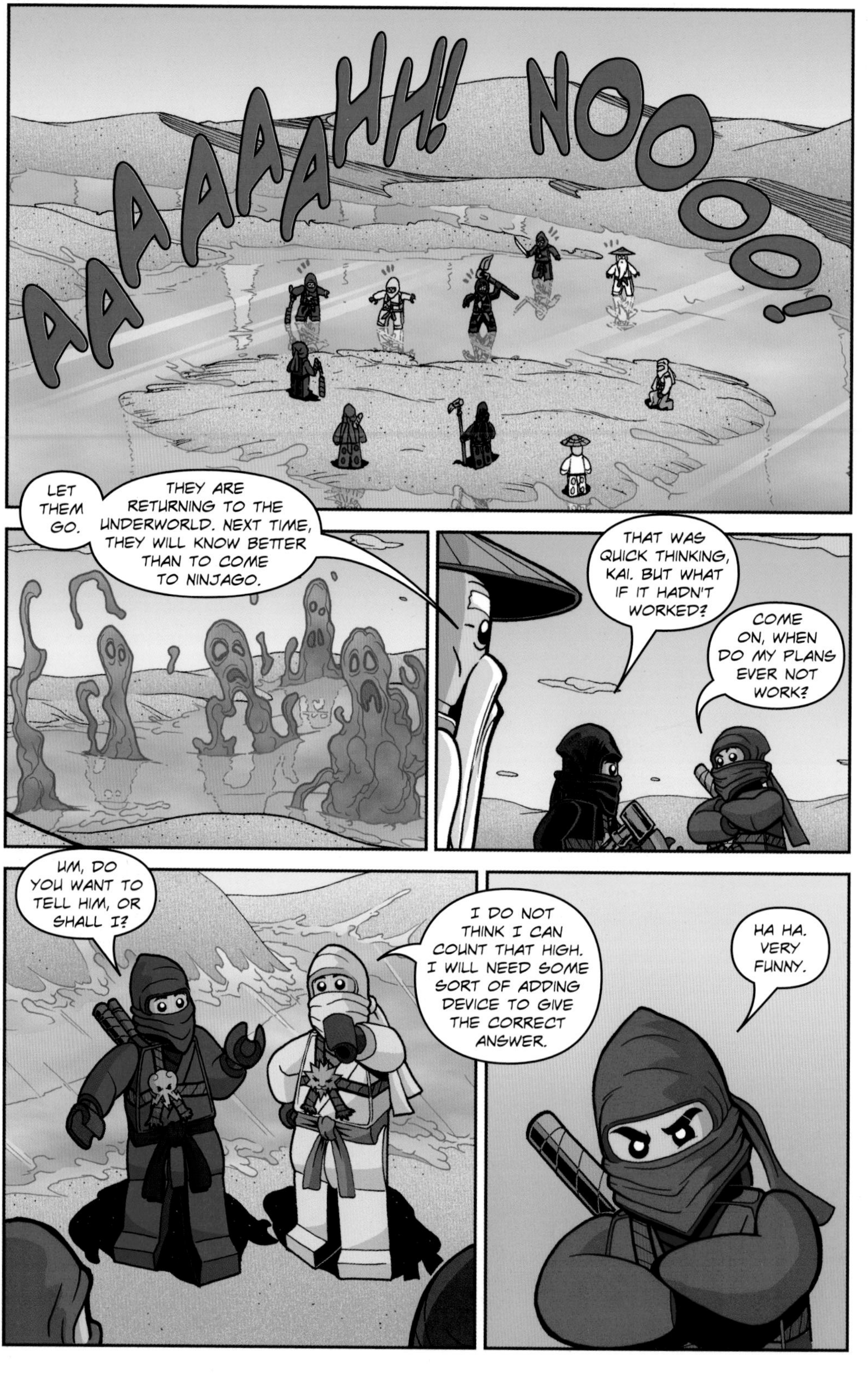
AAAAAAHH! NOOOOO!
LET THEM GO.
THEY ARE RETURNING TO THE UNDERWORLD. NEXT TIME, THEY WILL KNOW BETTER THAN TO COME TO NINJAGO.
THAT WAS QUICK THINKING, KAI. BUT WHAT IF IT HADN'T WORKED?
COME ON, WHEN DO MY PLANS EVER NOT WORK?
UM, DO YOU WANT TO TELL HIM, OR SHALL I?
I DO NOT THINK I CAN COUNT THAT HIGH. I WILL NEED SOME SORT OF ADDING DEVICE TO GIVE THE CORRECT ANSWER.
HA HA. VERY FUNNY.

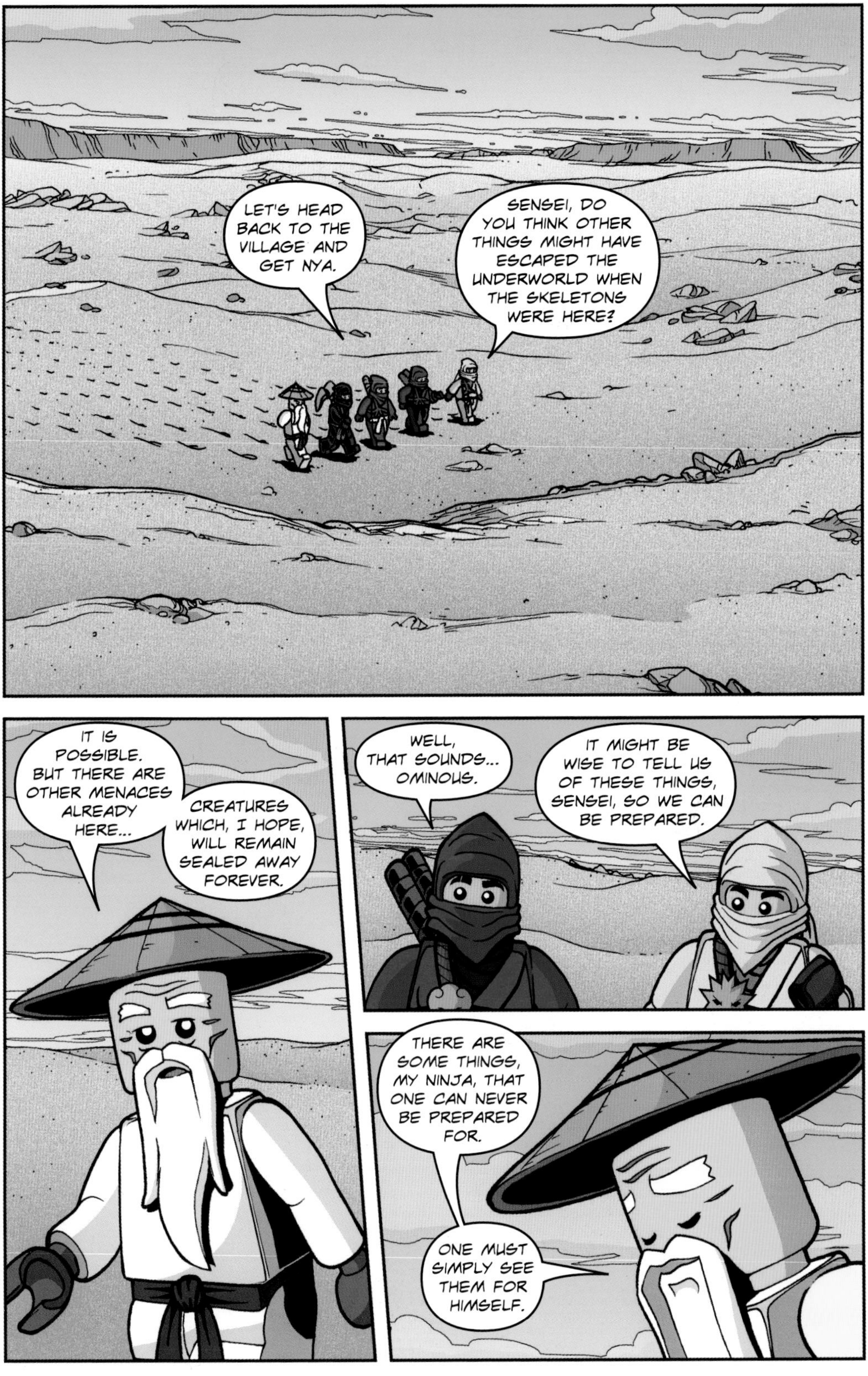
LET'S HEAD BACK TO THE VILLAGE AND GET NYA.
SENSEI, DO YOU THINK OTHER THINGS MIGHT HAVE ESCAPED THE UNDERWORLD WHEN THE SKELETONS WERE HERE?
IT IS POSSIBLE. BUT THERE ARE OTHER MENACES ALREADY HERE...
CREATURES WHICH, I HOPE, WILL REMAIN SEALED AWAY FOREVER.
WELL, THAT SOUNDS... OMINOUS.
IT MIGHT BE WISE TO TELL US OF THESE THINGS, SENSEI, SO WE CAN BE PREPARED.
THERE ARE SOME THINGS, MY NINJA, THAT ONE CAN NEVER BE PREPARED FOR.
ONE MUST SIMPLY SEE THEM FOR HIMSELF.

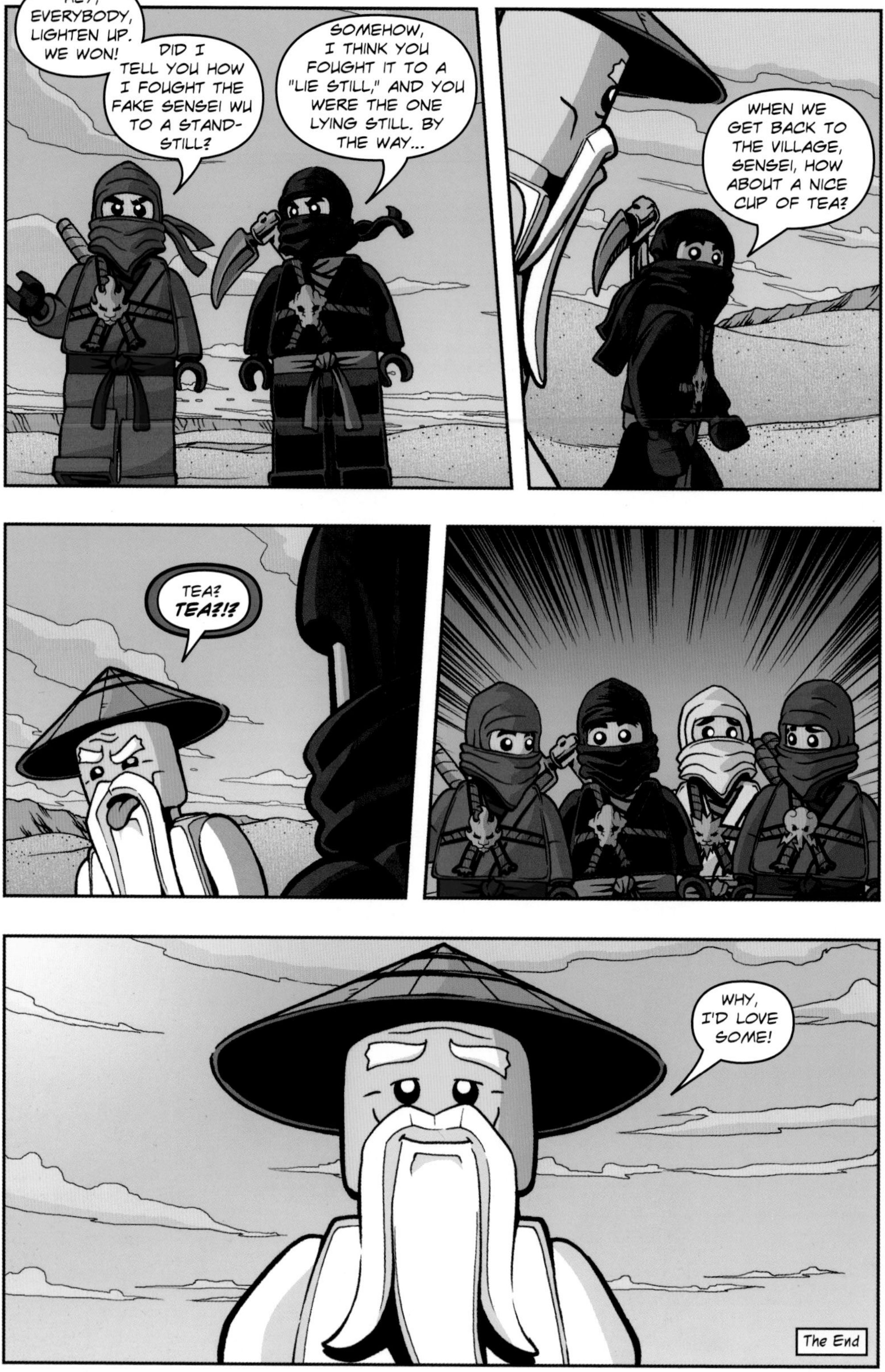
HEY, EVERYBODY, LIGHTEN UP. WE WON!
DID I TELL YOU HOW I FOUGHT THE FAKE SENSEI WU TO A STAND-STILL?
SOMEHOW, I THINK YOU FOUGHT IT TO A "LIE STILL," AND YOU WERE THE ONE LYING STILL. BY THE WAY...
WHEN WE GET BACK TO THE VILLAGE, SENSEI, HOW ABOUT A NICE CUP OF TEA?
TEA? TEA?!?
WHY, I'D LOVE SOME!
The End

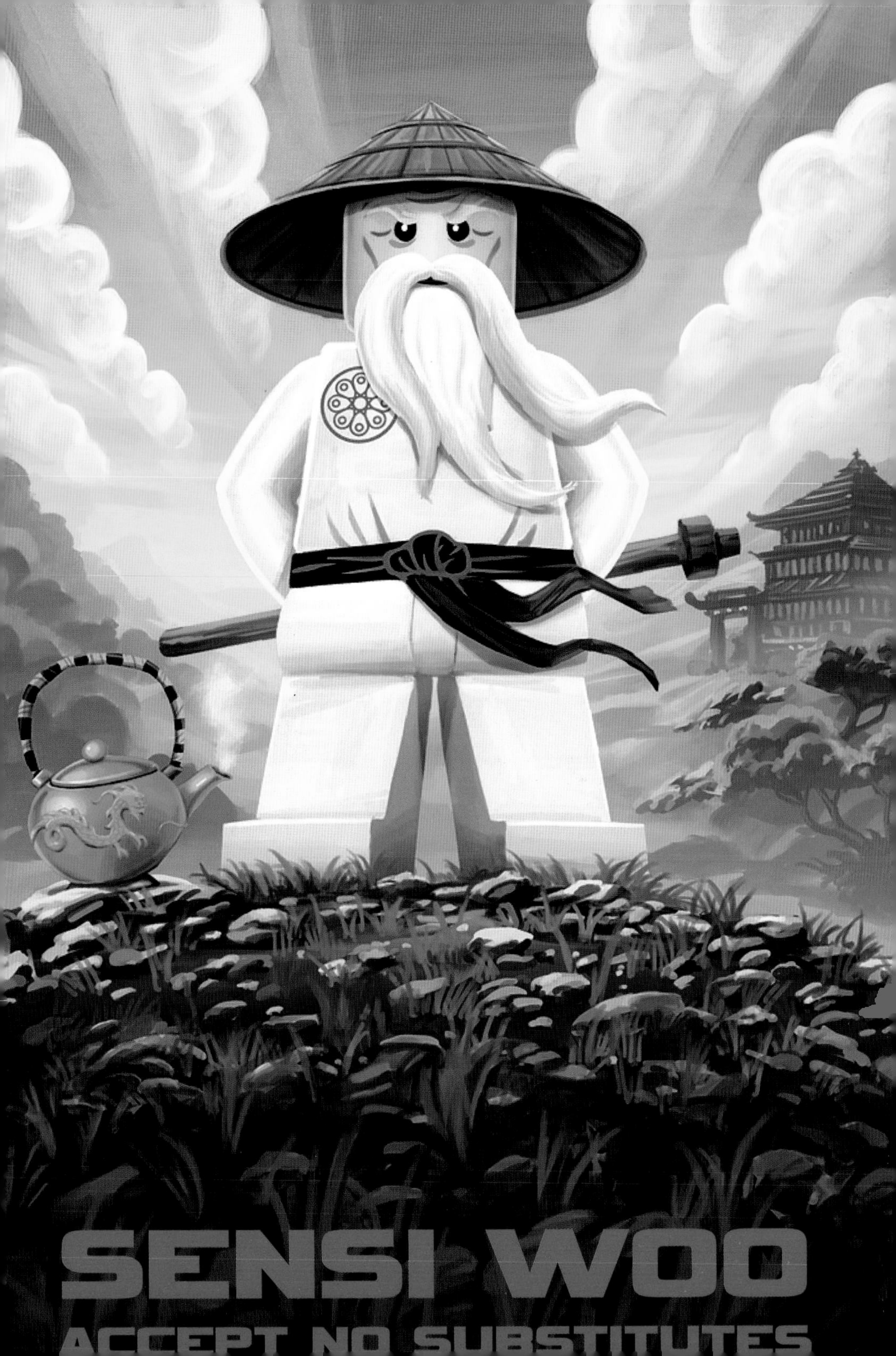
SENSI WOO
ACCEPT NO SUBSTITUTES

DON'T MISS THE NINJAGO MOVIE...

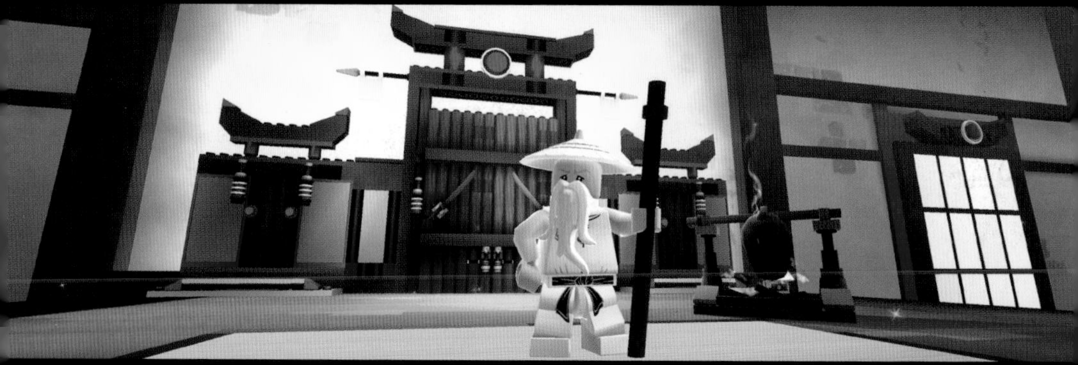

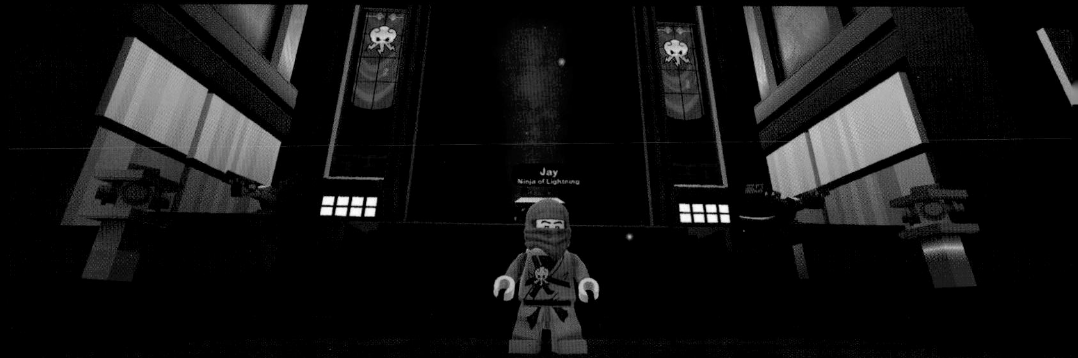
Jay
Ninja of Lightning

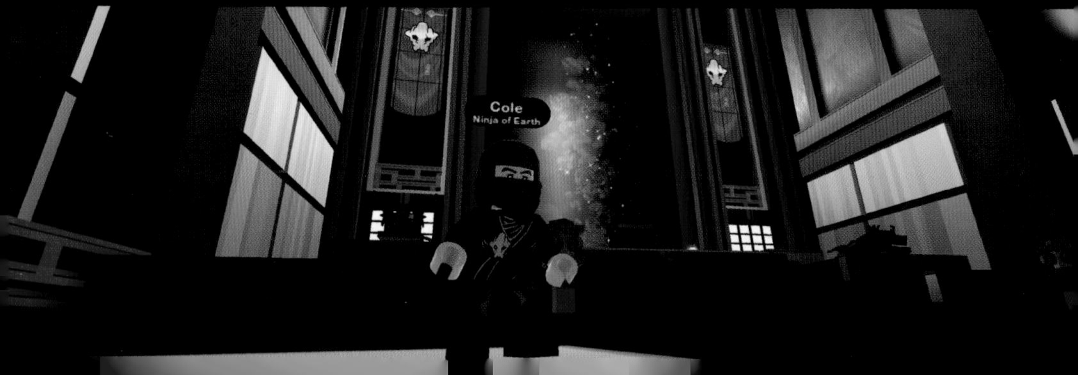
Cole
Ninja of Earth

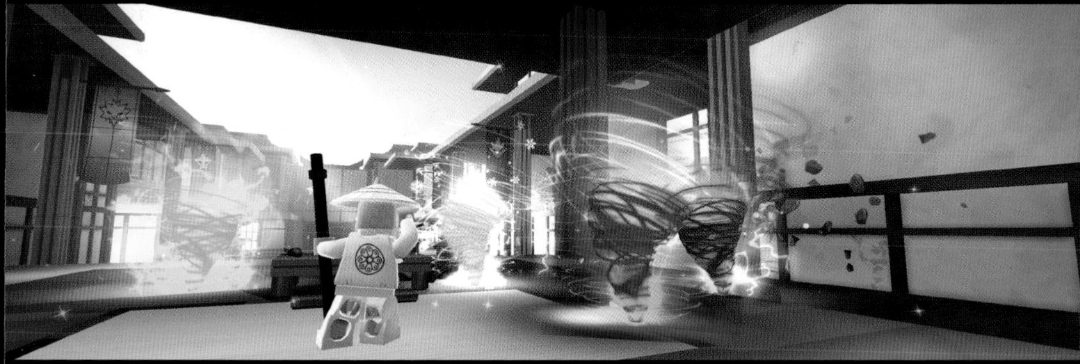

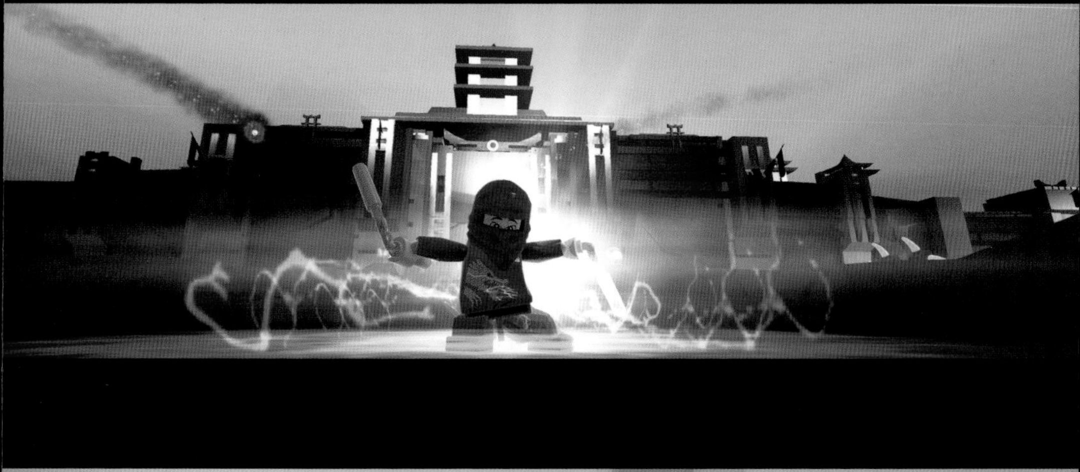

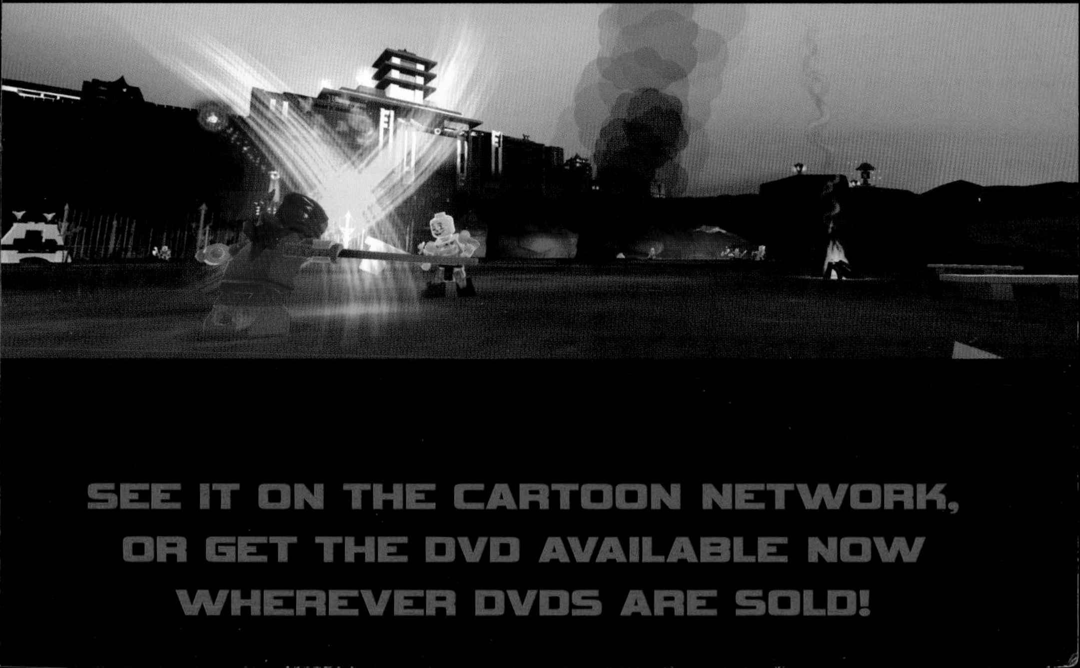

SEE IT ON THE CARTOON NETWORK,
OR GET THE DVD AVAILABLE NOW
WHEREVER DVDS ARE SOLD!

the SMURFS™

GRAPHIC NOVELS AVAILABLE AT BOOKSELLERS EVERYWHERE AND DIGITALLY FROM COMIXOLOGY.COM...

Graphic Novel #1

Graphic Novel #2

Graphic Novel #3

Graphic Novel #4

Graphic Novel #5

Graphic Novel #6

Graphic Novel #7

Graphic Novel #8

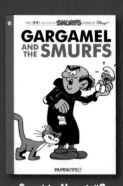

Graphic Novel #9

EACH GRAPHIC NOVEL IS 100% SMURFY!

WATCH OUT FOR PAPERCUTZ™

Welcome to the somewhat surreal second LEGO® NINJAGO graphic novel from Papercutz. I'm Jim Salicrup, the Editor-in-Chief of Papercutz, the company dedicated to publishing great graphic novels for all ages.

Before I go any further, I must take this opportunity to thank you for helping make LEGO NINJAGO one of the most successful graphic novel series ever published by Papercutz! We've had big hits before, with NANCY DREW, GERONIMO STILTON, THE SMURFS, BIONICLE® and even TALES FROM THE CRYPT #8 "Diary of a Stinky Dead Kid," but nothing has taken off in such a big way as LEGO NINJAGO. Fans obviously love Cole, Zane, Jay, Nya, and Kai and can't get enough of their action-packed adventures. And why not? LEGO NINJAGO features five friends having the most fun ever, as they work together to defend the world of Ninjago. It's exciting! It's dramatic! It's a well-written and well drawn adventure comic that stars the greatest ninja warriors ever constructed by LEGO!

And speaking of writing and drawing LEGO NINJAGO, we have a special announcement to make. But not before we thank both writer Greg Farshtey and artist Paulo Henrique for the incredible work they did on the first two LEGO NINJAGO graphic novels. Greg has not only done an incredible job of carefully crafting Ninjago stories, but he also is the writer of each and every BIONICLE graphic novel published by Papercutz. Paulo Henrique has been the regular artist on THE HARDY BOYS graphic novels for several years, and he's a master at designing dynamic comicbook pages featuring Frank and Joe Hardy. But after drawing LEGO NINJAGO #1 and 2, Paulo has decided to take on another Papercutz project—an all-new series featuring world-famous characters we're sure you'll love. While that's great news for this super-secret Papercutz project, what about LEGO NINJAGO? Who will draw it now?

Announcing the new LEGO NINJAGO artist—it's a man with plenty of comics experience. In fact, he's even drawn LEGO NINJAGO comics before. It's Paul Lee! So, be sure to join Greg, Paul, and me for LEGO NINJAGO #3 "Rise of the Serpentine," to boldly embark on a daring new direction in the lives our favorite ninja! Hey, we can't maintain our blockbuster status without you—so don't miss it!

Oh, and speaking of blockbusters (they don't call me segue Salicrup for nothing!), don't miss the original Ninjago movie on the Cartoon Network, or pick up the DVD-- available wherever fine DVDs are sold.

So, until we meet again in LEGO NINJAGO #3, remember to pay no attention to that man behind the curtain!

Thanks,

Jim